THE MAD MACHINES
OF MUNDARA

**The Third Book
of Dubious Magic**

For Rosco, Gregor,
and of course, Meredith.

With thanks to all my supporters at www.Patreon.com/Renoir
- especially Tegan McKechnie

CONTENTS

1 IF WISHES WERE LARGE GREEN MYTHOLOGICAL CREA-TURES

Three friends sat around a table after work in the *Punters Folly* tavern in Canberra – a pretty brunette woman, a Tasmanian man less tall than he'd like, and a shaggy haired man in a purple t-shirt. He was a wizard, but not many people believed him when he told them that.

The wizard was speaking, "It's like a little buzzing, somewhere deep in the back of my head. It doesn't go away. But with it comes the magic."

"Really?" the woman replied.

"Sorry Elizabeth. You know he gets like this after too many Scotches…"

The purple-shirted man tried to quash the interruption, saying, "Quiet, Wilko! You know the magic works – you've been there."

"I know weird stuff happens around you, that much I'll admit. But 'magic' is bull," snorted the Tasmanian – Robert 'Wilko' Wilkes.

Elizabeth Dance looked thoughtfully at the man in the purple t-shirt. He didn't *look* insane. A bit odd, but not mad.

"It started when I had that – accident. When I hit my head on the poker machine," the explanation continued.

"Yes," said Elizabeth. "You've mentioned that before." Perhaps a *little* crazy?

"Well, ever since, I've had this mystic power."

"Which is what, exactly?"

'To make attractive brunettes pay attention to you in bars, apparently' thought Wilko wryly.

Ordinarily there would have been several other friends and colleagues enjoying the bar with them, but their office was severely short-staffed. So the man in the purple t-shirt felt a little more freedom to discuss his unusual talent than he might in a larger, more sarcastic audience.

The wizard, John B. Stewart by name, scratched at his untidy curls as he admitted, "I really don't know how it works, but I wish for things and they happen."

Elizabeth nodded. "Yeah – I remember you mentioning that, too. Funny, I always thought magic was about making doves appear, or sawing women in half."

"Maybe I could," Stewart said with a shrug. "I've never thought to try."

"So what *do* you wish for?"

John B. turned his mind away from some recent dark moments in Central Australia and replied, "Simple things, mostly." He looked thoughtful. "I wish I had some barbecue crisps."

Wilko grumbled, "Alright, alright. I know it's my round." He called over to Beth the barmaid. "A Scotch, a schooner and a chardonnay please, Beth. And a packet of barbecue crisps."

As he crossed to the bar to pay for the order Beth was rummaging under the counter.

"Sorry, mate," she said. "I think we're out of… oh… wait. There's another boxful here… There you are – one packet of crisps."

"See?" said John B. moments later, offering Elizabeth a crisp.

"I'm not sure that's… really magic," she said uncertainly.

He shrugged. "Whatever it is, it works." He gave Elizabeth his best winning smile, and was pleased to have her smile back.

Wilko shook his head. "You shouldn't be trying to chat up a married woman, y'know mate."

Both Elizabeth and John B. scowled at him in annoyance. Stewart had drunk just enough Scotch to thoughtlessly exclaim, "I wish you'd get lost Wilko!"

The wizard caught himself and paled. "Sorry mate! I…"

"Nah, forget it, John. I deserved that. I know you both better than that, sorry."

Elizabeth smiled and said to Stewart, "He's still here."

John B. looked worried and replied, "So far."

Wilko was still there two rounds of drinks later. Then he hauled himself up from his chair and patted his stomach. "I must go and cast a portion of myself upon the waters of oblivion," he said.

"Pardon?" asked Elizabeth.

"I gotta go to the Gents."

"Ah," she nodded.

As the small man went she turned to John B. and remarked, "He doesn't seem worried about your magic."

"He should know better."

"Well, magically or otherwise, you got back from Central Australia safely. I admit I was worried when you left. And what about Scarlet! Who'd imagine Charlotte Burke deciding to hang out with a bike gang in Alice Springs? Some time I'd like to hear all about the trip," Elizabeth smiled.

"Not all of it you wouldn't. Scarlet seems to have discovered a new side to herself, yeah. And Wilko, well, he had his moments, I think. But some bits I'd rather not think about."

She looked at Stewart closely. He seemed to be serious.

Wilko meanwhile settled in a cubicle. He let out a long, contented sigh.

Then a drunk wandering out of the toilet turned out the lights. In sudden total darkness, with too many beers inside him, Wilko's co-ordination abandoned him completely. Cursing, he waited for someone to turn the lights back on. It was a long wait.

"If your magic really works," Elizabeth was saying, "I think you should wish for something really impressive."

"I've always had a feeling I shouldn't. There's an old saying, 'be careful what you wish for, it might come true'. With me it does, but not always how I meant."

"I understand," lied Elizabeth. "But it's a challenge! Why not wish for something really impossible, just to see what happens?"

"Like what?"

"Conjure up a dragon!"

"What if I don't believe in dragons?"

"Some people don't believe in magic, you know," she replied in a tone of voice that suggested she might be one of them.

It suddenly seemed important to John B. to convince Elizabeth Dance of his sincerity. "Alright," he said. "I wish a dragon would walk into this bar."

Nothing happened.

Stewart couldn't decide between relief and disappointment. Oddly, neither could Elizabeth.

Then they heard the tread of heavy feet and a scraping sound, like a large scaly tail being dragged down stairs. *Something* ducked through the doorway and lumbered to the bar. It was large, green, and looked very reptilian.

"Oh," said Elizabeth quietly as she put down her wine glass.

"Never thought of that," admitted John B.

They both smiled as the dragon appeared to reach up and pull its own head off.

"Jeez it's hot inside this outfit!" exclaimed the man at the bar to Beth as she approached him. "There must be an easier way to make a quid than tramping around in a dinosaur suit to advertise a bank!"

Elizabeth raised her glass to Stewart, laughing. "Okay, you won me."

John B. smiled back at her and said, "Thanks. I suppose I better go look for Wilko and make sure he's okay."

"Well, you're going where I can't follow by the sounds of it. This is probably a good time for me to head for home. See you in the office tomorrow?"

"Guess so. Will you be okay getting home?"

"Yeah, thanks. The lord and master doesn't get back from Sydney until Friday night so I'll take my time – grab a bite to eat on the way. Hey, do you want to… um…"

She looked in the direction Wilko had gone in. "Maybe not."

He smiled ruefully. "You've got a reputation to protect, mate. Last thing you need is anyone thinking you and I are anything more than friends."

As she stood up Elizabeth squeezed Stewart's shoulder affectionately and said, "I don't know about that. But good friends are hard to find. See you tomorrow."

Waving a hand in farewell the wizard bit down hard on any impulse to make any more wishes that evening.

.oOo.

2 A MAN DIES

One man sat in a comfortable padded chair. Another lay strapped down on something like an operating table. Both wore skullcaps of metal mesh, from which ran an array of wires which led to several machines at different points of a small room.

A single doorway led into the room. Opposite the doorway was a curved desk – the control panel for the array of machines. Behind the desk stood a blonde woman, her hand slowly turning a large silver dial. With high cheekbones and dark flashing eyes she was attractive in a way that was almost handsome.

The man in the padded chair exhaled a long, slow breath, as if waking from a refreshing nap. He reached up and removed the skullcap from a thick thatch of blonde hair. Despite chiseled features his bright blue eyes, long lashes and row of gleaming white teeth behind full lips made him attractive in a way that was almost pretty.

The man on the table didn't move. Not even a rise and fall of his chest. Nobody in the room cared what he looked like. He was dead.

The corpse's name was, or had been, Donald Northbridge. He was, or had been, something of a loner. Largely by choice, as Donald had always regarded himself as rather superior to everyone he knew.

It had been no surprise to him when an attractive blonde stranger had singled him out to flirt with in the bar he'd been visiting. One could hardly blame her, could one? He was a bit special, after all.

As a matter of fact, Donald Northbridge was a bit special. It was at a deep genetic level that the man himself didn't even know about. He would probably have been quite chuffed to discover that his DNA was out of the ordinary. The smug pleasure would have been diminished were he to have also been told that it was that same distinctive feature that led directly to his lying lifeless on a cold slab.

The woman wound the dial back to zero. Expressionless, she walked to the dead man and removed his skullcap. Her interest now in Donald Northbridge was pretty much zero.

"Success, Doctor?" she asked in a voice that carried a strong Eastern European accent.

The blonde man stretched and rose from the chair.

"Of course, Aleksa. My procedure has never failed since I – we – perfected it," he replied, his voice less strongly accented.

Aleksa bowed her head slightly in acknowledgement of his scant recognition. "I would ask Doctor, that I receive the next treatment," she said.

The doctor smiled a perfect smile. "I see no reason why not. I am feeling… refreshed."

"*Spaceeba.*"

"I thought you were determined to speak only in English since we came to this country? Old habits die hard, it seems," observed the man wryly.

"Indeed," Aleksa replied. "They die harder than men." Her voice was

casual as she undid the leather straps still binding the corpse.

"As you say. A pity so few, man or woman, seem able to survive more

than one or two treatments. Stronger subjects would be preferable."

The woman was about to protest but the doctor held up a hand and said,

"I know you are doing the best you can with the resources available, and it

is enough. For now. Time is with us Aleksa, always with us. Better stock

will present itself, I am sure. Meanwhile, Gleb can dispose of this one

off the south end of the island. The sharks there are voracious feeders, it

seems."

As they left the room the doctor favoured Aleksa with another of his per-

fect smiles and said, "Perhaps it is the environment here, hah?"

.o0o.

3 MATTERS OF CHOICE

Kaiser Ron looked around the small meeting room and sighed sadly. Managing this motley crew was a challenge at the best of times, and today was not the best of times.

Christened Ronald Mark Kaiser, he was long since used to his nickname, and was used to having a certain amount of difficulty with his staff that'd coined it. But the last few weeks had been bloody ridiculous!

Charlotte Burke – an odd bird right enough, but one of his most dependable business analysts. Suddenly she takes it into her head to take indefinite leave and stay in Alice Springs. Hanging around with a motorcycle gang, he'd heard by rumour, but that was just too silly for words, surely.

Yes, alright, Wilkes and Stewart had come back from their holidays last week, but just in time for *four* others to go off on sick leave.

When the memo had landed on his desk instructing him to immediately send two analysts to Melbourne to conduct testing of a new program before it was installed nationally, he'd thought, 'This is the last straw! Now I'm expected to take two more out of what's left of my team – who's going to do all the work round here? Me?!?'

So the team meeting had been called. Ron ran has hand through his hair, and cursed silently at the sticky gel catching his fingers. His wife the hairdresser had been experimenting on him again, and while his new look added somewhat to his height, he knew it added nothing to his dignity.

He explained the new program, and the testing regime that had been asked of them. Reluctantly he asked for volunteers to go south to write hypotheticals, work out parameters, push figures and data through the new program and analyse the results.

"Anyone? Anyone at all available to fly to Melbourne tomorrow morning?" he asked.

"I'm up for it boss," offered John B.

The manager looked at the scruffy figure, wearing yet another of the seemingly inexhaustible supply of purple t-shirts. Was this the image of his team he wanted to convey to the stuffed shirts in Melbourne? Did he have a choice?

"Okay John," he said, trying to conceal his reluctance. "Anyone else? Please?"

Elizabeth raised a tentative hand. "I suppose, at a pinch? Sonny can manage without me when *he* travels for his work. I'm sure he can manage if *I* have to go for a bit."

"Mm – I'm not so sure I can manage without you," admitted Kaiser Ron.

Jeff Masterman spoke up. "I could go, Chief?"

The boss shook his head. "You're a programmer, Jeff. I need an analyst to run the tests and document the results, sorry. Wilko, what about you?"

The Tasmanian looked uncertain. "I don't know Ron – I've just got back from the trip up to the Centre. I'm not that much of a traveller…"

"It's not a holiday. There's work to be done," Ron reminded him.

John B. grinned at the prospect of travelling with one of his best mates again.

"It's okay buddy, I'll look after you in big bad Melbourne," said Stewart genially, slapping his friend on the shoulder.

Wilko rolled his eyes. "Great," he muttered.

"Alright then, you two fly out as early as you can tomorrow. Go sort out your travel and accommodation. Better still, get Elizabeth to help you – she's good at this sort of stuff. I'll give you the outline of the testing plans and you can start working out the detail this afternoon."

As usual, Ron had to fight down the urge to finish the meeting by saying 'Class dismissed'.

*

A few hours later, an even smaller group than the previous week had convened at the *Punters Folly*. It was a group of two, to be precise – Elizabeth Dance and John B. Stewart.

Wilko was still in the office, fretting over the testing plans for his allotted part of the project.

"It's his nature," John B. observed. "He'll recheck every detail a dozen times."

"Not like you, hey?" Elizabeth replied.

"Nope," admitted the wizard. "Check everything twice and leave it at that. You look too hard and you'll start seeing things that aren't there."

"Like dragons."

"Ah, but we did see that one, remember? You're not staying late tonight, I suppose."

Elizabeth's face showed a smile but there was unhappiness behind it as she said, "No, I wish I could, but Sonny's home and he's being a pain."

"How so?" asked John B.

"He's always so *angry*," she explained.

Stewart looked surprised. "Really? Never noticed that in the couple of times I've met him."

"He's good at being charming in public. He just bottles the anger up and lets it out again in private," Elizabeth said, with her smile dissipating completely.

"What's he got to be angry about? He's got a good job, he's married to a beautiful woman…"

The smile returned, with genuine warmth this time as she responded, "Thanks. He's been angry since he was a kid, I think. It started with his name."

"Really? What is his real name?"

"Just what you know – Sonny Dance."

The wizard wasn't sure whether he should laugh or not. "Sonny? I thought it was a nickname. He was actually christened Sonny Dance?"

Elizabeth nodded and sipped at her wine. "Yep. Afraid so."

"Jeez – talk about a Boy Named Sue. Was it supposed to toughen him up I wonder? Some parents can be unkind, eh?"

John B. saw the unhappiness in her eyes and attempted to lighten the mood. "Good thing he didn't have a sister – they'd have probably called her 'Moon', eh?"

Elizabeth just looked at him, lips tight.

Stewart put down the glass he'd been about to drain of Scotch and said quietly, "Oh. Oh dear. Poor girl!"

"I think she changed it just as soon as she was old enough. She'd already run away from home by then."

"So why didn't Sonny do the same thing?" asked John B.

The unhappy Mrs. Dance shrugged. "It's complicated. Lots of reasons – there was a time when I thought I respected them. I don't think much of any of them any more. Stubbornness is a big reason. And like you said, maybe the stupid name toughened him or at least made him think so. And he's absolutely devoted to his mother. She chose the name and he wouldn't do anything to upset her."

This time the Scotch was drained, but the wizard didn't signal to order another. "I wouldn't have picked him as the type. I presume Mum approved of the marriage?"

"Didn't disapprove, at least. And to be fair, for the first few years it was pretty good. His temper just seems to have been getting worse lately." She saw Stewart's expression darken and laid a hand on his arm. "It's okay. He hasn't touched me. It's just not very nice to live with."

Determined to try to be positive John B. rested his hand on Elizabeth's, smiled and said, "Things will work out for the best."

Elizabeth tried to look convinced but failed. "Hmph. I'm starting to think I should expect the worst and never be disappointed. Hope is just the first step on the road to disappointment."

Stewart shook his head. "*Believe* in the best, and it *will* ultimately happen. Just keep the faith."

Elizabeth drained her wine glass, patted the back of his hand and said, "I'd better head for home. I hope you're right."

John B. gently squeezed her hand and replied, "I believe I am. I wish you happiness, pretty lady."

As he looked at her sad smile he thought to himself, 'The tricky bit is knowing what's best.'

.o0o.

4 WORDS WITH FRIENDS

John B. had left the *Punters Folly* very soon after Elizabeth. His mood

wasn't light, and he knew that if he headed straight for his regular seat at

his other regular bar – the Daramalan Devastators Football Club – he'd

make a long stay of it. That would probably mean unnecessary stress

when trying to pack for a week or two in Melbourne.

 Packing was not ordinarily an issue for him – the majority of his ward-

robe comprised jeans and a lot of purple t-shirts. But Melbourne's weather

was notoriously fickle. Locals would simply advise, "If you don't like the

weather stick around – it'll be completely different in a little while." So

throwing at least a couple of long-sleeved t-shirts and a rainproof jacket

into his kitbag seemed shrewd.

'Better go home, do it now and get it out of the way,' he'd thought as he

went to board the bus.

 It was a short trip to the cottage John B. shared with two of his closest

friends. He called to one of them as he opened the front door.

"Kat! Food!"

 A loud cheerful "*Rraoww*," came from the lounge room in reply.

 Kat was a large white Persian cat. His response to Stewart's call was to

uncurl himself from the armchair where he'd been drowsing, stretch, scratch behind his ear so as to leave just a little more fur on the chair, then jump down and pad leisurely into the kitchen to be served the promised food.

There's an old saying that cats don't have owners, they have staff. The relationship between Kat and John B. was far more amicable than that – they were clearly friends. At times a casual observer might wonder which of the two was unsure of his species. At times the answer to that might be 'either'.

Stewart took some leftover beef bourgignon from the fridge, spooned a substantial helping into Kat's bowl, then microwaved it just enough to bring the meal to slightly above blood heat.

The big Persian waited patiently for his bowl to be placed before him, and gave a gracious "*mrreah*" of thanks before burying his face in the food.

John B. turned his attention to his other housemate.
"Darren!" he called. "You home?"

Darren James Bond was a tall skinny young man – the young brother of a former University mate of Stewart's. He'd come to Canberra in search of a future, or at least some direction towards it. So far he'd found what might diplomatically be called 'adventures' in the outback with John B., and a series of jobs in takeaway food stores.

Darren, fortunately, was an equable soul who took the slings and arrows of life with good humour. He still played war games for amusement (though rather less often than he used to) and still regularly went into the back yard to practice using some of his weapon collection.

This still occasionally disconcerted some of the neighbours who happened to glance over the fence. Darren's weapons included nunchakus, a pike, and a few different swords.

When not describing graceful curves through the air in Darren's surprisingly skilled hands, the weaponry was arranged in and around Darren's room.

First time visitors to the cottage were invariably bemused by Darren's 'room', which was actually the space under John B.'s dining table. A very large and decorative bedspread, piles of books, and the aforementioned weaponry formed 'walls'.

Stewart knocked politely on the table, wondering if Darren was asleep on the light mattress under there. No reply. The wizard was puzzled for a moment, before a samurai sword resting on an edge of the bedspread caught his eye.

'Ah, that's right!' he thought. 'It's his first night in the new job! He's working at the front counter of the Japanese restaurant up the road. I'll pack, walk up to the restaurant and have a word, then catch a cab out to the Club from there.'

Kat's amiable greeting had done much to lift John B.'s mood. Packing was quickly finished, and after a minute or two's indulgent scratching between feline ears, the wizard was soon enjoying a brisk walk to Darren's new place of work.

The "*Mojo Tojo*" touted itself as selling "the coolest Japanese food in Canberra". What this meant in practice was a fairly standard range of sushi and a few other Japanese standards, served in a venue decorated in late-1960's San Francisco chic. The restaurant was adorned with lots of tie-dyed wall hangings, bead curtains and brass fittings.

"Nice place you've got here," John B. observed to his housemate upon arrival, finding the young man standing behind a display counter painted in fluorescent rainbow colours. A Jefferson Airplane album was playing on the *Mojo Tojo*'s in-house sound system.

"It's not so bad at night when the lights are dimmed. Otherwise it can hurt your eyes a bit," Darren replied with a grin. "You want something to eat?"

"One of those plain salmon sushi rolls to take away, please mate. It'll tide me over till I get to Devastators. But I wanted to let you know, in case I didn't catch you in the morning – Kaiser Ron's sending me to Melbourne for a week or two. Wilko and I are working on a new program the Department's installed in a test site down there. Would you mind looking after Kat while I'm gone?"

"No worries. It's not like he's any trouble. Melbourne, eh? Never been there. Like most of Australia I guess, but I'll get there some day."

John B. laughed lightly. "Glad to hear all that carry-on in the Centre hasn't put you off seeing the country," he said.

"Nah. Weird, scary sometimes, like when we were trying to get out of that cave-in, but no – it hasn't put me off going places and seeing things. I wouldn't mind a job like yours where I'd get to travel now and then."

The wizard shook his head. "Darren old buddy, I'm not sure I'd wish my job on you. You've got a healthy imagination and I'd hate to see it stifled in the smothering embrace of Public Service bureaucracy."

"You manage alright," the young man pointed out. "I don't want to spend the rest of my life cooking and serving different varieties of junk food."

"So what do you want to do?" Stewart asked.

"The honest answer is – I dunno yet."

John B. reached over the counter and clasped his friend's shoulder, saying, "Well, I wish for you that you'll find something that you're good at that makes you feel fulfilled and happy, and lets you be just as busy as you want to be."

Darren grinned back at him. "That sounds good – thanks mate. Now, did you want wasabi with that salmon roll?"

"Spare me! I want to be able to taste the salmon. Keep the change," he said as he handed Darren a ten dollar note.

"Thanks mate – my first tip!"

"Here's another one. Follow your instincts. Okay – if I don't catch you later tonight or in the morning, I'll see you when I get back!" said John B. genially as he picked up his sushi.

"Okay. I'll keep Kat company till then!"

The wizard and his housemate exchanged cheery waves as Stewart left

Mojo Tojo. If they could have foreseen coming events their mood would have been less casual. But then, John B. had never wished to see the future.

.oOo.

5 TESTING TIMES

It was a different city and a different bar, but the same routine.

Curiously, the bar was called '*The Capital*'. That was curious because Melbourne was not the national capital (although it had been considered for the title over a century earlier). There were a number of locals who still argued that had been a mistake that needed correcting.

When asked, the bar owner would explain that *The Capital* was a very sensible name for a bar in the financial district, and there was certainly some truth in that. But for a couple of regular Canberrans – residents of the country's *real* capital - the potential irony of making the bar a 'home away from home' was irresistible.

It was one of the few times since their arrival in Melbourne a week earlier that Wilko and John B. had been able to sit down and enjoy a drink after work together. The nature of the testing regime that had been devised was such that both of them were working long hours, but they were mostly working to quite different timetables.

Kaiser Ron was happy with the results he'd been receiving. If he'd physically been present there he would have been pleased (and in John B.'s case perhaps surprised) at the commitment to the job they were showing.

"It's coming together well, mate. I reckon we should be done in another couple of days," observed Stewart, raising a Scotch in salute.

Wilko raised his beer glass in return. "Yep. Better than expected."

"Ah, but that's because you always expect the worst," said John B.
"Expect the worst and never be disappointed. The worst you can be is
proved right."

The wizard shook his head. "You sound like Elizabeth. And you don't
have the lovely Sonny to contend with."

Wilko looked surprised. "Things not good at home for her?" he asked.

John B. shrugged and replied, "Apparently not. None of my business I
suppose. Just a bit concerned. As a friend."

"Of course." Wilko was genuine, any teasing gone in their shared fondness for their friend and colleague. "But as you say, none of our business
unless and until we're asked, eh?"

"Right enough."

They clinked glasses together and sipped their drinks, looking idly
around the bar.

"Y'know, I think she's got her eye on you," observed Wilko quietly.

"Who? Elizabeth?" asked Stewart in sudden confusion.

"No – that blonde sitting on her own over there," said the Tasmanian. He
discreetly indicated with a tip of his glass the direction his companion
should be looking in.

Stewart glanced over as casually as could manage. Sitting alone at a
table was a blonde woman. All he could take in during a quick glimpse

was that she was well made up without looking overpainted, had dark eyes
– striking rather than pretty, hard to pick her age. Her attention seemed to
be focused on what he took to be the mobile phone in her hand.

"Must be a text message, she looks like it's something special," was the
wizard's comment.

"She was looking straight at you a minute ago, mate, with the same look
on her face."

John B. laughed. "Coincidence, old buddy. That's all."

"Yeah, well, that'd make more sense, wouldn't it?" agreed Wilko, sharing
the laugh. "I'm going to head off after this beer," he advised. "My next
packet of data's coming through at nine tonight, and I want to be in the
office ready for it. I've worked up some stuff that'll give the new system a
real workout."

"Oh, good. That'll probably generate some fun and games. I hope you
haven't made life too hard for our poor guinea pigs, they're doing their
best to make it work, you know."

"I know, mate. But you know as well as I do that we've got to figure
out the most extreme scenarios possible. They're the ones that'll test the
system good and proper, because let's face it, the real world will throw up
some weird stuff."

There was a smile on Stewart's face, but there was a serious undertone in
his voice as he said, "I reckon that the 'real world' is capable of produc
ing far weirder stuff than your imagination, old buddy. But your theory

is sound. A big day ahead of us, I fear. I probably won't stay long after you. I promised I'd sit down with some of the data process staff first thing tomorrow to look at a couple of their questions and that was before I knew you were going to be brightening their world. They all seem to start before seven thirty. I'd forgotten there was a seven thirty in office time!" complained Stewart, mostly in jest. Mostly.

Wilko laughed, drained his glass and waved a vague farewell as he strolled out of *The Capital*.

Left to himself, John B. ordered another Scotch – the last for the evening, he told himself – and looked around the bar, trying to spot a television that was showing a sports broadcast. Any sport would do.

To his considerable surprise he turned back to find Wilko's recently vacated bar stool suddenly occupied by the blonde they'd noticed earlier. "Good evenink," she purred.

John B. raised his glass in polite acknowledgement. "Good evening to you," he replied.

"Aleksa," the woman said, smiling and holding out her hand.

Stewart returned the smile, and on impulse took the proffered hand and kissed it gallantly.

"John B. Stewart," he said. "Can I get you a drink?"

Aleksa's smile widened. "That would be lovely – thank you."

Stewart gestured appropriately to the barman, who evidently recognized the woman as he promptly poured and delivered a shot of vodka.

"Cheers," said Stewart, raising his glass.

"*Dost* – er, your health," Aleksa replied, and clinked her glass against his.

"You are new here, yes?" she said.

"Pretty much – yeah. Been in Melbourne about a week. And you? You don't sound – ah – quite like a local"

She smiled and said, "No – I live south of here."

John B. chuckled and replied, "Funny, I'd have put your accent rather more to the north. South of here – Tasmanian?"

"Not quite. I live on a little private island."

Impressed, Stewart raised his glass. "Nice!" he said. "What do you do for a crust that lets you own your own private island?"

It was Aleksa's turn to chuckle. "No darlink, I do not own it. I work there, and for the most part I live there. But it is a little dull, so I come into the town sometimes. For – amusement."

The wizard looked around the bar. "I'd have thought there'd be better options for amusement than the *Capital*. Nice enough place for a quiet drink, but not what I'd call exciting."

"Ah – but it is people that I find interestink. New people, especially. Such as you, darlink – tell me about yourself."

A little alarm bell went off in the back of Stewart's head, but despite his reservations he smiled at the implicit flattery.

"Nothing all that interestink – interesting, sorry," he demurred. "Just a humble public servant here to do some singularly uninteresting work.

Well, uninteresting to most people – I'm working with a mate who I'm afraid might actually be enjoying it."

"The small fellow who was drinkink with you?"

"Yeah. Wilko. As good a mate as a bloke could wish for, but takes life a bit more – seriously than I do."

"Ah, you see – already you are more interestink than you give yourself credit for. A man who does not take life too seriously, that is good."

Aleksa turned slightly so that light flashed off the large dark gem in the pendant she wore, catching Stewart's eye.

"You like it?" she asked. "It is called saturnine." As she spoke she moved slightly so that reflections of light danced across his eyes.

"It's very – dark," he replied. "I'm more of an amethyst man, myself."

He blinked and shook himself slightly. Aleksa made a mental note to herself.

"So, you were tellink me about yourself. You have family?"

"Was I?" John B. shook his head slightly again, as if trying to clear it.

"Family? Well, parents, obviously. Long gone now, God rest 'em. No one else, I'm afraid."

The Russian woman rested her hand lightly on his. "That is surprisink," she said. "A little – unfortunate for you, perhaps."

Their eyes met. She seemed sincere.

"Thanks," said the wizard.

To his surprise, and perhaps disappointment, Aleksa suddenly drained the last of her vodka and stood up.

"I must go, I am afraid, darlink. You will be here again tomorrow eve-nink?"

John B. shrugged and said, "Not certain. Work might be a bit messy tomorrow I suspect. How about the day after, for sure?"

Surprising him again, she leaned and kissed his cheek. "That would be good," she said. "Perhaps I can buy you the drink I owe you, yes?"

"Perhaps. I don't keep score, especially with a lady," Stewart grinned, stood, and gave a small gallant bow as Aleksa walked away.

She stopped in the door of the bar, looked back and gave him a final smile and a wave before going out into the street.

John B. sat back down and decided to order himself another Scotch. 'Well, you never know your luck in the big city, as the saying goes,' he thought to himself, still grinning.

Outside, Aleksa had taken from her pocket the small device that Wilko and Stewart had mistaken for a phone. She looked again at the figures on the display she'd brought up on screen.

'It is so much better that there will be no one to miss him,' she mused.

'Still, with these readinks I do not think that Doctor Solo will care.'

Moments later a large ugly man walked out of the *Capital*. Without a word he stood beside the blonde woman and folded his arms. She showed him the display on the apparatus in her hand. His brow furrowed.

"This is… unusual, *da*?" he said.

"Yes, Gleb. Unusual, and very promisink."

The smile she wore as the two of them got into a convenient taxi was very much colder than the one she'd earlier given to John B. Stewart.

.oOo.

6 SOMETHING GOES WRONG

It was two days later. The intervening day had, as John B. had feared, been something of a shocker at work.

The new data that Wilko had input the night before had created a number of surprising and complicated errors, which the data processing staff duly added to their list of questions for John B.

It had taken several hours of research, analysis, data modeling and trial-and-error to answer most of the questions, but a few were proving especially stubborn. Despite lengthy consultation with Wilko, working well into the evening, and right across the following day, a couple of questions remained unresolved by the time Stewart was ready to say, "Enough!" and head for the *Capital* to meet Aleksa.

Wilko had already packed it in for the evening, and begged off from drinks citing a desire for an early start in the morning.

Stewart had been just about to pick up the phone in the testing centre and call Kaiser Ron in the Canberra office to 'escalate the problems' when he noticed the time.

"Oh bugger – I didn't realize it was that late!" he said to himself.

He checked the paperwork he had with him, hoping for an after-hours number. No such luck. Then a little flash of inspiration struck him. He had Elizabeth Dance's home number written in his pocket diary. Given how much the Kaiser relied on her administrative skills there was a good chance that she'd have Ron's number.

The wizard smiled a happy little smile to himself as he dialed.

The phone in Canberra only rang twice before Elizabeth answered it.

"G'day pretty lady," said Stewart in reply to her 'Hello?'

"John B. here – sorry to bother you, mate, but I was wondering if you had Kaiser Ron's number at home. Got a problem here that Wilko and I can't fathom."

"Um… no, sorry mate. Give me the details and I'll give them to him first thing in the morning."

"Yeah – that sounds like the best idea. I've had enough of this. Time I went for a drink."

"Bad day? You poor baby," Elizabeth said laughingly.

Then John B. could hear an indistinct voice calling to her in the background. He assumed, correctly, that it was Sonny.

"Is everything okay?" Stewart asked.

Elizabeth's voice was non-committal. "Yeah, I suppose so."

Sonny's voice was more clearly audible down the phone as he shouted, "Queenie – where are you?"

"I'm on the phone – be with you in a minute," Elizabeth replied, with as much politeness as she could muster.

Her husband barked, "Who you talking to? Get in here!"

"In a minute, I said."

Despite some concern at the tone of the exchange he overheard, John B. couldn't suppress a chuckle.

"Queenie? He calls you Queenie? Queen Elizabeth – I get it. Not bad, as nicknames go. How about if I…"

"Don't you dare!" she snapped. "He's the only person who's ever called me that."

Stewart was contrite. "Special, huh?"

"Maybe, once."

"I like the idea of a nickname on you, though. And it's more interesting than Liz or Betty."

"I got 'Liz' or Lizzie at school, and all the lizard gags that went with it. And ugh – I hate 'Betty' – the name should have been outlawed when The Flintstones finished!"

"Queenie…!" Sonny's shout was louder.

"Hang on, I said. It's a work call. John, I'll talk to Kaiser Ron in the morning, but I'd better go."

"Sounds like it," said John B. "Hey – how about Q? As in QE2?"

She chuckled. "That's kinda nice. Funny thing is, my maiden name is actually McKew."

"Q it is, then," the wizard said with a smile in his voice. "Sorry, mate, you're stuck with it now!"

He couldn't see her chew her bottom lip slightly then grin as she said,

"Hmm – alright." There was a pause before she said quietly, "Listen, please be careful there, okay? I've got a bit of a bad feeling."

"It's Melbourne, it's business, and it's boring. That's all. No demons, no fish-gods," replied Stewart.

"Eh?" The references meant nothing to Elizabeth. At work Stewart hadn't shared much detail of the trip to Central Australia, and while he'd been in the midst of it all, Wilko still was adamant he didn't believe in magic. The Tasmanian certainly wasn't about to start chatting casually about demons and ancient gods.

The wizard dodged the issue. "Stories for another time. Thanks for worrying, but I'm fine," he said.

"Okay – but I wish we could be having this conversation in a coffee shop or a bar somewhere, not over the phone," she said, something like coyness in her voice. Softly she continued, "I'd… like to actually see you."

John B.'s reply was similarly quiet. "Yeah. Yeah, I'd like that too. It's a nice wish. You take care of yourself too, alright? I'll be back soon. Thanks, Q."

"You're welcome. Take care, John."

"You too, pretty lady."

"Queenie!" Sonny roared, obviously from quite near the phone.

"Must go John, I'll discuss the question with Ron in the morning," said Elizabeth formally before quickly hanging up the phone.

Stewart looked at the phone pensively as he put down the handset. "I hope I haven't just made a bad situation worse," he mused.

Then he looked around the working papers strewn about the desk, sighed and sorted them into a few cursory stacks.

"Tomorrow," he said to the piles of problematic work. "Tonight, there's a lady who reckons she owes me a drink, if I'm lucky."

*

John B. was, in truth, a little surprised when Aleksa greeted him as he walked into *The Capital.*

He had no reputation as a 'ladies man' in Canberra. He had friends who were female, but had never been known to have a girlfriend as such, and while he showed cheerful interest in attractive women he was never an active pursuer. Neither had he been known to be actively pursued by any-one, attractive or otherwise, male or female.

John B. was scruffy rather than ugly, but neither was he especially attrac-tive.

"Nothing special," was how he would quite reasonably describe himself. All of which meant that Aleksa's apparent interest in him was a nice but unexpected change.

"Good evening, ma'am," he said with a grin as he approached the bar and gave an old-fashioned bow.

Aleksa was nonplussed for a moment. She hadn't been addressed with such chivalry for – a long time. It had long since ceased to be a feature of her working environment.

"Good evenink, sir," she replied after a moment, and smiled.

As if sensing her momentary hesitation, a man sitting on his own at a booth in the corner of the bar looked up and glowered.

Catching sight of him from the corner of her eye, Aleksa gave a small gesture of reassurance that went unnoticed by John B.

"I had thought perhaps you were not comink after all, darlink," she purred.

Stewart shrugged and said, "Sorry I'm a bit late. It's been a bugger of a day at work."

Aleksa signaled to the barman for a vodka and a Scotch. "This is how you cope with a bugger of a day, yes? A drink or two?"

"Or three, or four, depending on how much of a bugger it's been," he admitted cheerfully.

"Well, here is your first."

They raised their glasses and clinked them together.

"To the future," she said.

Stewart nodded. "A nice toast. To the future."

His first Scotch disappeared at a gulp, a fact that Aleksa noted with interest. She sipped at her vodka rather more demurely, and waved agreement that John B. should get a drink for himself.

They made small talk about Melbourne weather, and talked in very non-specific terms about feeling undervalued in workplaces that they'd been in.

As Stewart drank, at about three times the rate of his companion, she kept carefully moving so that light reflected off her saturnine pendant and glittered into his eyes.

Eventually she said, "After such long days, and now the whisky, you must be tired, darlink."

"Actually, no," he replied. "This is the best I've felt in days. Just the break I needed, I think – good whisky and good company." He raised his glass to her.

Her smile was a little thinner as she answered, "Thank you."

She downed her vodka a little more quickly and stood up.

"I think I would like to take a little fresh air," she said. "You will join me, yes, darlink?"

"Eh? Oh, sure. Of course." John B. took the hand Aleksa offered and allowed himself to be led out onto the street.

"Foolish perhaps, I suppose," she remarked. "I ask for fresh air, and find I am wantink a cigarette. Let us step out of this breeze."

They took a step into an alley beside the bar. The wizard positioned himself as a windbreak, his back to the street.

Aleksa withdrew a slim silver case from her pocket, selected an elegant black cigarette and rolled its gold filter delicately between her fingers before putting it to her lips. She proffered the case to John B.

"Black Russians – I haven't seen those for ages!" he exclaimed. "Very appropriate, milady, but I'll pass, thank you."

Stewart's eyes were on the cigarette case as Aleksa closed it. He'd completely failed to hear footsteps – his first inkling that there was someone behind him was the thud of a pistol butt against the back of his skull.

It was only the hardness of that skull which prevented him from being knocked cold. As it was, he landed heavily among the alley's litter and rolled groggily onto his back.

"I am sorry dat vas necessary, darlink," said the blonde, smiling down at the wizard.

John B. looked at his assailant, who was also looming over him. The man wasn't a pretty sight. He was a large fellow – reasonably tall but with a physique like a steamed pudding. His complexion might be described as lunar, and the pockmarked face was topped by a shock of black hair that could have been wrung out to fix a squeaky door. There was a moustache. It looked like it had been drawn on in heavy black marking pen by a particularly clumsy three-year-old.

"He will co-operate now I think, *da*?" offered the big man.

Stewart's gaze went from one to the other and back. 'Please let him not be named Boris,' he thought. 'If either of them says "Shoot little squirrel!" then I know I'm dreaming.'

"You are a difficult man to put to sleep," said Aleksa with something like a sad sigh.

"Always thought… it was impolite to… fall asleep… on a lady," Stewart managed to reply.

The large ugly man kicked him in the head, hard, and the wizard lost his tenuous grip on consciousness. Aleksa sharply struck the big man's shoulder with the back of her hand.

"Gleb, you fool! If you've damaged his brain the Doctor will be furious!"

"Pah! What makes this one so special?"

"I do not know precisely what, but you saw his scan results. They alone make it clear that somethink certainly does make him special! Doctor Solo made that plain when he sent us to obtain him so urgently. Now quickly, pick him up and make it look like he is drunk, while I hail us a taxi!"

With a surly grunt, big Gleb hoisted Stewart up by an arm, which he then draped over his shoulders to hold the unconscious wizard upright. Light rain started to fall as he waited for Aleksa to attract a cab.

John B. didn't notice.

.o0o.

7 A COVER STORY

Darren could hear Kat inside the cottage as he walked up the couple of steps to the front door. It wasn't a *mew*, it was more like a wail, and it had been clearly audible from the footpath.

That was unusual. The big Persian wasn't normally a loud cat, except for his purr. Darren hurried to open the door.

The cat sprang past him and stood on the Welcome mat, his tail flicking rapidly in obvious agitation. Almost as quickly his head turned from side to side as he looked up and down the street.

The yowling which Darren had heard as he approached was replaced by a much quieter strange *eh-eh-eh* sound which seemed to quiver in time with the flashing tail.

Darren knelt to stroke Kat's back. The cat didn't move away, but wasn't obviously calmed, either.

"What's up, mate?" asked Darren. "I'm sorry I'm a bit late home from work, but I did leave your dinner out for you."

After a final long look up the street, Kat turned and went back into the cottage. His tail was still twitching, and he was still quietly making the odd noise that sounded like muttering.

Puzzled, Darren followed the cat through the doorway. There was con siderably more white fur than usual on the carpet just inside. Clearly Kat had been waiting there for some time.

The young man closed the door, then made his way into the kitchen.

Kat was lapping from his water bowl, beside which his food dish was still half full.

Darren observed this with concern.

"Whatever's upset you must be big, to put you off your grub," he mused aloud.

*

As the following day wore on, Wilko was also becoming increasingly upset. The glitches in the system appeared to have finally been resolved, and the testing process looked to be nearly over, but it would have been nice if John had been there to help with the finishing touches.

The Tasmanian had been surprised when Stewart hadn't appeared in the breakfast room of the Regal Hotel where they were both staying, but assumed that the previous night had turned into a big session in the *Capital*, which was being slept off.

When his old friend still hadn't turned up at work by late morning Wilko had started to grumble. He covered for the absence, explaining to the Melbourne staff that Stewart wasn't well. Maybe the Melbourne weather wasn't agreeing with him? That wasn't uncommon with visitors to the city.

During his lunch break he went back to the hotel, but no amount of knocking on Stewart's door raised a response. He returned to the office, his emotions torn between annoyance and concern.

He knew John had a certain amount of history of overindulging his fondness for single malt whisky. It was certainly possible that he might have decided to raise a glass to the impending end of the job, and that one glass might have led to a few more. It wouldn't be the first time Stewart had missed a day at work after too many whiskies. But it was unlike him to not at least call in with a lame excuse that nobody believed.

Maybe, implausible as it seemed, John had 'got lucky' and was happily ensconced with some woman somewhere. That blonde in the make-up, the one with the mobile phone the other night, she'd certainly seemed to have her eye on him. But really – John B. Stewart? Wilko couldn't imagine it. Or if he tried to, he immediately tried not to, and vigorously scrubbed the image from his mind.

All of which left him with 'concern'. Melbourne was an unfamiliar city for both of them. It was bigger, louder and more cosmopolitan than Canberra, or Hobart or even Brisbane – earlier homes for him and his friend respectively.

It was certainly possible that something grim had happened. Recent events in Central Australia hadn't made a lot of sense to Wilko, but he did at least know that the world wasn't necessarily the safe and predictable place he'd grown up believing in.

When he made his afternoon report to Kaiser Ron he discreetly avoided any mention of John B.'s non-attendance.

At the end of what would otherwise have been a satisfyingly conclusive working day Wilko set off for *The Capital*. He was hoping, almost expecting, to find his old friend propped at the bar, a glass of single malt in hand.

No such joy. There were a few people in and at the bar, some of them by now quite familiar faces.

Wilko gave a nervous grumble, then ordered a beer and sat at the bar, more in hope than expectation.

It was just less than an hour later when Aleksa and Gleb arrived at *The Capital*.

*

As Aleksa predicted, Doctor Solo had been less than impressed by the force that Gleb had used in subduing John B. the night before.

"All your training, all your *practice*, and yet you quieted this man by battering his skull like a football. I despair of you sometimes!" the doctor had railed at the pock-faced man.

Getting only sullen silence in reply, he continued, "How bad was the voyage back here? Could he have sustained more damage?"

Gleb shrugged. "No worse than usual. The strait is never calm."

So throughout the day the doctor had monitored Stewart's condition carefully. He kept his guest gently sedated while he conducted a battery of tests using a range of machines, most of which would never be found in any self-respecting hospital.

By mid-afternoon he was sitting in a comfortable chair in his parlour, his pretty blonde eyebrows arched as he read the test results.

"My dear Miss Yusupova, you do not disappoint me. These results completely corroborate the information you first brought to me."

Standing by the mantlepiece, Aleksa raised a fine crystal tumbler that contained a generous measure of very, very good vodka.

Solo continued, "I had wondered at first whether the scanning device had been in error, but clearly this is not so."

"I am gratified, Doctor, that you thought to doubt the equipment and not me," she replied.

She was favoured with a dazzling smile.

"Had I cause to doubt your skills you would not be here today, would you?" he said breezily.

The doctor was clearly in a good mood. He waved a leisurely hand toward Gleb, who occupied a less comfortable chair. Another fine crystal glass of vodka looked incongruous in his meaty paw.

"That is true of you too, my old friend," Solo said. "I owe you a measure of apology – our guest seems quite intact. It should be said that we may owe that good fortune to his possessing a skull that is somewhat more robust than the average. Still, that is one of the least of the remarkable characteristics he displays.”

Gleb’s first reply was a grunt, then, as if realizing his ungraciousness, he raised his glass.

“Thank you, Doctor,” he said. “If he is so impressive, perhaps we may *all* partake…?”

Solo’s languorous hand movement stiffened into a gesture of resolve.

“This one is *mine*,” he answered sharply. But then he looked once more at the test results on the paper in his hand, and seemed to regain his good humour.

“I think there may be sufficient left when I am satisfied for you both to receive some consideration of your own.”

Aleksa and Gleb raised their glasses and smiled. There was nothing good in those smiles.

Doctor Solo stretched with a look of pleasure, flexed his long fingers and rose from his chair.

“I shall go downstairs and make certain that Mr. Stewart continues to be secure. You two are to return to the mainland and ensure that this col-league of his will not soon miss him. By the time you return we should be ready to begin treatment.”

*

After surveying *The Capital*'s interior the blonde gestured to her unattractive companion to take up his usual position in the corner of the room. Then she glided up to the bar and sat on the stool beside Wilko.

"Good evenink," she purred.

" Um… g'day," said Wilko, fumbling for words. "I've – um – seen you here before, haven't I?"

Aleksa shrugged. "I come here quite regularly. Their vodka is good. Would you like a drink?"

Wilko's mouth opened and closed a few times before he could coherently say, "No thanks. I just bought myself one. Would you - ?"

"Oh, how kind! A small vodka, please. What a charmink impression of a small fish you do!"

The Tasmanian blushed uncharacteristically as he ordered the shot of spirit.

Aleksa continued. "Thank you," she said, lightly touching Wilko's arm.

"You're welcome, Miss, or should I say Ms.…?"

"Yusupova. Please, call me Aleksa. And you are?"

"Robert Wilkes. Er, my friends call me Wilko," he replied, awkwardly holding out his hand to be shaken.

Instead she simply held it for a moment, squeezed lightly then released it.

"Speakink of friends, Weelko, have I not seen you here with the shaggy haired fellow? The one dressed in purple?"

'Ah-ha!' the Tasmanian thought. 'It bloody well was John she was eyeing off!'

Aloud he said, "Yeah. John. I work with him. Sorry – he's not around tonight. Don't know where he is."

He was surprised when that was greeted with a smile.

"So I have the pleasure of your company to myself," the woman replied.

"Um… yes. Thank you. I'm a bit worried though. Our job's pretty nearly finished and I reckon we could be leaving tomorrow, but I haven't seen him all day to tell him."

Again she lightly touched his arm and said, "It is good of you to be concerned, but I am sure he is secure somewhere. Put your mind at rest, you will hear of him soon. Let us talk of other things – Melbourne is not your home?"

Aleksa moved slightly on her stool. She continued to do so as they made small talk about the Melbourne weather and how much it resembled their respective original homes. All the while, light reflected from her saturnine pendant and flickered across Wilko's face.

He dimly noticed that his eyelids were getting heavy, and his brain fuzzy. 'I haven't had that much to drink, have I?' was almost his last thought before a heavy dark curtain draped over his conscious mind. Yet he didn't fall from his bar stool, and his breathing remained regular without the distinctive snoring generated when he slept.

Aleksa leaned and spoke softly into his ear. "Listen to me, Weelko – and remember this. You have spoken to your friend John today. Work was a bugger for him, and a lot of drinks would help him cope. He would stay in another place, a cheap hotel here in Melbourne for some more days, until he felt better. He said to you, 'Nothink to worry about, all is fine.' You are to go back to Canberra without him. Remember this!"

She turned to briefly nod to Gleb. The big man looked disappointed. Then Aleksa squeezed Wilko's arm sharply.

"Weelko! Are you alright?" she asked sharply.

The Tasmanian came to with a start, blinking as he looked around.

"Sorry! I must have just – vagued out for a moment there!" he apologized.

Patting his arm, Aleksa said, "It is alright. It has been difficult work, yes. A – bugger – as you say?"

With a rueful smile Wilko replied, "At times, yeah." His face clouded. "That's what John said. That's why he… he… needed a few drinks. Yeah. He's… staying on here for a few days." He shook his head, as if to clear cobwebs. "Up to me to tell the boss, I suppose."

"Your boss, he will understand, yes?"

"Kaiser Ron? I don't know if 'understand' is the right word, but I don't reckon he'll be surprised."

Wilko struggled to suppress a yawn. "Sorry," the small man apologized again. "I don't know why I'm so tired all of a sudden."

"It is alright, darlink. I think you just need to sleep now."

Moving cautiously, Wilko got off his stool. "I think you're right. Good-night Ms. – Aleksa. Thanks for your company."

She squeezed his outstretched hand and replied, "It is I who should thank you. You have been most – obliging. Good night, Weelko. Sleep well."

The Tasmanian wasted no time in returning to his room. Once there he kicked off his shoes, sat on his bed to unbutton his shirt and promptly toppled sideways, asleep before his head hit the pillow.

Within seconds, the many and varied sounds of his snores were reverberating through the wall. That night Wilko slept far more soundly than the unfortunate traveller in the next room.

.oOo.

8 CROSSED WIRES

52

John B. had spent the day slipping in and out of consciousness. He didn't slip very far in. The first few times that he did, he was mostly aware of nothing more than a throbbing headache, then once or twice a sharp pain in his arm as a needle was jabbed into it.

Time passed. At one point he became dimly aware that he was having trouble moving. He was on his back – couldn't roll over, couldn't sit up…

Tied down – that was it! Tied or strapped. That didn't seem right. He could turn his head, and he struggled to make sense of his surroundings. Difficult when nothing seemed to be in focus.

A hazy figure in white appeared beside him. Then there was the sharp pain in the arm again, and everything sank back into darkness.

Sometime later some consciousness again gradually returned, like a bubble slowly making its way up through a dense liquid.

It took Stewart some effort to open his eyes. The effort was first rewarded by the glare of a light bulb suspended from a white ceiling. Wincing, he turned his head to the left.

There was a woman standing beside him. She was wearing a white coat. 'Not another needle!' was his first thought, rapidly followed by 'Where do I know that face from?'

The blurry figure of the woman moved and he realized that it wasn't a needle she was holding. Something bigger – a wire basket of some kind?

His mind was clearing faster than his eyes, but it was a race between snails.

He felt a chill on his scalp, then a lot of unpleasant prickling. It was wire mesh shaped into a cap.

"Everythink is ready, Doctor," came the voice of the woman, now out of view above his head.

He knew the voice. The accent. Alice someone? Alicia? Aleksa – that was it!

At the same moment that sliver of recognition crossed his mind, so did another jolt of pain as electrodes were pushed into his scalp.

John B. turned his head the other way. The movement was uncomfortable but achievable.

His eyes began to focus properly. Across a small room he saw a fresh-faced blonde man sitting, apparently at ease, in a comfortable chair. The man was wearing a fine mesh skullcap of his own.

To Stewart's surprise, the man gave him what seemed a cheery wave and a smile that revealed perfect white teeth.

'He looks like a model,' thought John B., even as he knew what a peculiar notion that was.

He'd just started to realize that the smile and the gesture weren't directed at him when he heard Aleksa's voice again, now from the far side of the room.

The last sounds he heard were the words "Commencink transfer," and a rhythmic metallic noise.

Stewart sank into unconsciousness like an aeroplane descending into heavy cloud.

Such cloud always contains turbulence. Sometimes it hides mountains.

*

The rhythmic metallic sound – it was an engine. A motorcycle engine. An antique – yes, a World War 2 vintage Ariel, and the engine was laboring somewhat as the bike churned up a large sand dune.

He was in Central Australia. Riding to Alice Springs in the bike he'd been lent by… by… an old black guy, yes.

Wow, must have started to doze there. Dangerous, when riding way out here. Still, it wasn't surprising that he was tired and drained. It had been stressful. Going out into the desert to find… to find… a scientist, no – an archeologist. That's right.

The bike crested the dune, and he allowed it to freewheel down the other side.

He rolled to a halt and let the engine idle. It must be the sun. He didn't feel quite himself, all of a sudden. The sun and the stress could do that to you.

And of course it had been stressful, even though at the time he'd been too busy, too caught up in the moment, to actually register that. Someone had tried to kill him with the venom of a dead snake – it had nearly worked.

And someone else… a madman, yes, had tried to turn himself into a god using a human sacrifice and something weird, ancient… what were the details?

There was a sudden commotion beside him. From the sidecar? Yes, the Ariel had a sidecar. A big white cat – of course, it was Kat – jumped out of the sidecar onto the sand. The bike wasn't moving so he was taking the chance to use the enormous sandbox that was the desert.

John B. wiped the sweat from his forehead. 'You need a bloody good sleep, Konstantin,' he thought to himself, then pulled himself up short. Where did *that* name come from?

Kat had finished his ablutions, and the rider idly watched the plume of sand the cat was flicking into the air. The quite graceful arc the sand described as it flew through the air.

He watched as the particles of sand showered into the grave. Sand? No, not sand – earth. Rich, brown, still damp from the recent rain.

The tall, dark-clothed man beside him put a consoling hand on the youth's shoulder.

"You bear up well, Konstantin," the man said. "The Count would be proud of you."

He frowned, but found he could not reply. He'd been staring at the earth as it steadily covered his – father? – yes, his father's coffin.

Now he looked up, and looked around. There was a small, respectful crowd gathered but there seemed to be, somehow, less than there should be.

He struggled for words. "Where…?" he began haltingly.

"They have not turned up – even now, neither of them. Your older brothers are a great disappointment to many of us in the Tsar's court."

'Brothers? I have older brothers?' The thought tumbled around in his head, looking for a memory to anchor itself to. He was struggling to concentrate. Grief. That must be it. Grief was playing tricks on his mind.

That was annoying. He had been training his mind.

"It is my view," the Royal Court official continued in his sonorous voice, "that it was the profligate ways of your brothers which, at least in part, led Count Dashkov to his grave before his time."

"Yet – I have been… provided for…"

The older man failed to notice the puzzled tone of the youth's voice. "Indeed," he replied. "I myself would have preferred your education to have been in the arts – three generations of Dashkovs have shared their love of beauty with the Imperial Court. But so long as your brothers have, nominally at least, followed the paths expected of them, the Count saw fit to let you have your way in studying the sciences. He told me before he died how proud he was of your efforts. You have an 'ambition for knowledge' he told me."

The young man swayed unsteadily on his feet. "Ambition. Yes. I will fulfill that," he mumbled, and closed his eyes, savouring the comforting darkness.

*

The darkness parted like storm clouds. John B. opened his eyes, looked up into the glare of the ceiling light and closed them again.

His head felt full of cotton wool, but so full that it hurt. He could hear voices – one male, one female, speaking agitatedly. He couldn't make out what they were saying.

"*Kto-nibud' gavarit pa-angliyski?*" he asked.

There was only silence in reply, as Aleksa and the barely-wakened Solo looked at each other in shock.

"*Shto*?! Er – what?" gasped Aleksa softly.

"Does anyone here speak English?" repeated the figure strapped to the table.

Aleksa leaned to whisper in the Doctor's ear as she helped detach his skullcap, "A side effect of the treatment? We know he's… unusual."

"Perhaps, perhaps." Solo looked distracted.

"Are you well, Doctor? Was the treatment – unsatisfactory?"

"I think… perhaps… Mister Stewart shall prove more challenging than – anticipated. Still, well worth it…"

"More difficult than our recent subjects?" asked Yusupova.

Doctor Solo twisted and stretched uncomfortably as he rose from his chair. "More than any subject – recent or otherwise, I wonder. But never let it be said that Konstantin Solovyov would not, or could not rise to a challenge!"

.oOo.

9 SHOOTING THE MESSENGER

Wilko was feeling more than usually put upon. It wasn't his fault. *He* knew it wasn't his fault. Other people knew it wasn't his fault, and usually admitted that. Later. After he'd borne the brunt of their anger.

Kaiser Ron had been first.

Wilko now had a new understanding of the term 'hair trigger temper'. Ron's wife had been experimenting on his hair the night before. Again. This time she'd been experimenting with both shape *and* colour. Neither had worked.

Repeated washings that night, and again in the morning, had succeeded only in removing some of the gel and the most incandescent of the colour.

The Kaiser was acutely aware that he'd arrived at work looking very like a big yellow porcupine had settled on his head.

The first person to come into his office had been Wilko.

From a technical perspective, the news from Melbourne had been good. The testing of the new system had gone well, and there would be a full rollout soon after the appropriate reports were written and signed off.

One of those reports was supposed to come from the testing team of Wilkes and Stewart, and now here was the Tasmanian half of that dynamic duo advising that his partner had gone Absent Without Leave.

"What do you mean, the stress got to him?" demanded Ron.

Wilko looked embarrassed and not a little baffled.

"I'm only telling you what he told me, Ron, sorry. The work was getting him down, and he needed a few drinks. So he decided to stay on in Melbourne for some more days, until he felt better."

The boss shook his head. "You shouldn't have accepted that. I wouldn't have. You should have hauled him back here with you by whatever means necessary!"

Wilko couldn't even begin to express how unfair, unreasonable and downright impractical this was. His mouth opened and closed a few times, but no sound came out.

"I need the testing report, and I need it as soon as possible. You'll have to write it yourself since Stewart can't drag himself out of a pub somewhere in Victoria," the Kaiser fumed. "Well don't just stand there – go and get on with it!"

The reaction of workmates Jenny Farmer, Davie Harris and 'Tinkerbell' Hardman weren't as belligerent a Ron's but neither were they especially sympathetic.

"Mate, you should've stayed with him and made sure he was alright," said Tinkerbell, who needed little coaxing to join someone in a bar himself.

Londoner Davie conceded that it might not have been the wisest strategy to join in the truancy, but was adamant when he said, "Droppin' the poor bugger into trouble wiv' the Kaiser was a black act, but. You coulda just said 'e was crook or something."

"But I'm just repeating what he asked me to say!" Wilko protested.

Jenny shook her head. "Even so, you could have done better. We all know what John can be like when he's had a few too many. The whole 'I can do magic' routine springs to mind. You might have looked after him better is all I'm saying."

Wilko was at a loss to answer that one. Over the course of their travels in South Australia and the Red Centre of the country he'd come to appreciate that John B. Stewart, for all his eccentricities, was quite capable of looking after himself.

So he said as little as possible to anyone else for the rest of the day, quite glad to have the testing report to immerse himself in. He mused to himself that the only saving grace was that Elizabeth Dance wasn't at work that day. He suspected her reaction would have been even less friendly.

The next morning he found that gloomy thought to be absolutely accurate.

Of course, Wilko wasn't to know that the reason Elizabeth hadn't been at work was that she was moving out of the house she shared with Sonny. Her husband had heard her say, 'I'd like to actually see you' during her phone conversation with Stewart, and had leapt to a paranoid conclusion.

The resulting huge weekend-long argument was, as Q put it later, "the final bloody straw, but y'know I'm actually *glad* of it." She'd spent Monday moving a few things into a small hotel room until she could work out an alternative, preferably without alerting the office rumour mill.

But it did mean that she wasn't in the best of moods on Tuesday morning. That mood was not helped when the first thing she did at work on Tuesday morning was answer the phone ringing on John B. Stewart's desk.

It was Darren on the line, agitated that his housemate hadn't returned from Melbourne and hadn't sent any message to say he'd been delayed there. So the young man had rung the only work number he knew – Stewart's own.

Elizabeth did her best to be reassuring, despite being armed with absolutely no knowledge of what was going on. Her next move after hanging up the phone was to rush to Kaiser Ron's office and ask if he knew anything about where Stewart might be.

Neither Ron's demeanor nor his tonsure were markedly improved from the morning before and his only explanation was a waspish retelling of Wilko's brief story.

Then she descended on Wilko's desk like a thunderstorm in a gale. "What's this bull about you leaving John behind in Melbourne?" she demanded.

Tinkerbell and Davie exchanged looks and decided that this was a very good moment to pop outside for a cigarette.

Wilko raised his hands defensively. "It's like I told Kaiser Ron," he said. "Work was being a bugger for him, and he figured a lot of drinks would help him cope. He decided to stay in a cheap hotel here in Melbourne for a few more days, until he felt better. He said to me quite specifically, 'there's nothink to worry about, all is fine,' and I was to go back to Canberra without him."

"And you've heard nothing since. And neither has anyone else."

"Well… I…"

"Not even the bloke he lives with who just rang here. He's heard nothing at all. Not even from you."

"Darren?" Wilko was genuinely puzzled. "I assumed John would have called him."

"Well you know what the first three letters of 'assume' are, don't you?" said Elizabeth angrily.

By now Wilko was getting tired of feeling put upon. "Listen," he said, with some heat in his own voice, "I'm getting fed up with people having a go at me because John's taken it into his head to go on a bender. It's not like he's a teetotaler who's fallen off the wagon, is it? I mean, he's got form!"

Q and Wilko glared at each other.

"He's supposed to be your mate. You might have looked out for him," she said.

"How well do you know John?" came the reply. "You think he's going to listen to anyone telling him what to do? Especially when it comes to drinking?"

"So you wipe your hands, then clear off home and leave him to take his chances in some crappy pub in a strange city. Great."

"He's a big boy, Elizabeth. And the place we were staying in was quite okay."

"I know – I processed the booking forms and the payment, remember? That's part of my job. But you reckoned he was moving into somewhere cheap. There's some really rough dives in Melbourne."

Wilko paused for a moment. For an instant, something had felt wrong, but he was too irritated at being made to feel like the villain of the piece to think it through.

Instead he replied, "I know that. I also know that over the years John's been in and out of quite a few rough places. I reckon he knows how to look after himself. If he wants to go hide in a whisky bottle for a while, well, I might not like it any more than you do but it's his right. And none of our business."

Elizabeth intertwined her fingers and tapped her thumbs together for a moment. She knew that Wilko was fundamentally right, and that she wasn't being entirely fair to him. She knew her nerves were frayed after the row with Sonny, and she'd been looking forward to a quiet talk with John B. Stewart far more than she'd let on even to herself. His unexpect-ed absence was a blow, and she wasn't well positioned to take a blow that morning.

"Alright," she said grudgingly. "We'll just have to wait for him to get in touch, I guess. Sorry I snapped your head off."

"Yeah, okay. Look, I know it's a bit odd, but he'll be fine. He said so himself."

"And that's a comfort, is it?" she asked with the trace of a grin.

Wilko returned the softened expression and replied, "Not really, but I suppose we trust him, eh?"

Both slightly mollified, they got on with the morning's work. Wilko finished the testing report, 'ghost writing' John B.'s share. They had, after all, shared the work and the results, and discussed both at length in *The Capital*.

'Funny,' the Tasmanian mused to himself as he wrote. 'All the time we were working on this he didn't seem especially stressed. I thought he was actually enjoying the exercise, at least a bit.'

Perhaps some of that thought infused itself into the report. Certainly, as Elizabeth Dance proofread the document that afternoon she gleaned some sense of his doubt from between the lines.

Somehow it raised again concerns that she had only vaguely felt that morning then laid to rest after the confrontation with Wilko.

The proofreading was done in less time than Kaiser Ron might have deemed appropriate. The rest of the afternoon she spent making telephone calls and taking notes.

Shortly before Ron left work quite late in the day Elizabeth cornered him in his office.

"I've been looking at the reports on the new system. It looks pretty good, but there's one thing missing," she said.

The Kaiser rolled his eyes and said, "Oh no – what?"

"I think that there needs to be some feedback from the people who were actually using it, not just the two testers," she replied.

"Wilko and John did say everyone seemed okay with it," Ron observed.

Elizabeth gave a nod that contrived to look doubtful.

"I was just thinking that you wouldn't want to risk anything like awkward questions, or worse, resistance from the union when it comes time to introduce the system nationally."

"Well, no… obviously not…"

"If we can get some actual comments from the system users in Melbourne, get them to sign off that they were happy with it – that should prevent any trouble."

"Can you just ring a few of them?" asked Kaiser Ron, seeing her reasoning but unsure of where it was leading.

Q shook her head. "I don't think that would be good enough if we were to strike a cantankerous union delegate."

"Yeah, well, there are a few of those in this Department," Ron conceded.

"Exactly. I've had a thought. I can go down to Melbourne and run a couple of focus groups. Talk to the users – make sure they really are happy and get them to say so officially. If they're not we can find out why and sort out the problem – whether it's technical or just a lack of understanding or poor communication or whatever. Better now than when the whole system goes live."

The boss nodded. It all made perfect sense.

"But does it have to be you that goes?" he asked, not wanting to lose his unofficial office manager.

"I thought it might be best if it was. You and I both know I've got the skills and experience in that sort of work."

Again Ron had to concede her point. Elizabeth had come to the Department from a very prestigious private company that she'd only left because Sonny had constantly complained about the extremely long hours she'd worked.

She'd had some sympathy for her husband's concerns in those earlier days. The job had certainly required a lot more than regular nine-to-five hours and she'd been genuinely extremely busy - not having the affairs that Sonny always suspected.

"Fair enough," said the Kaiser. "How long do you reckon? A day?" he asked hopefully.

"I thought I'd spread the focus sessions over three days. I'd like to take a bit of time over each session, and not take too many people away from their normal jobs at any one time."

Ron sighed. Again the suggestion was entirely reasonable and he couldn't argue with it.

"One more thing," Elizabeth began.

Ron almost winced. "Yes?" he said.

"I think I should take Wilko with me. He can answer any technical questions they throw at me. Well, most of them, I expect."

"That makes sense, yes. Is he okay with the idea?"

"He will be." Q's tone of voice made it clear that Wilko would be okay with the idea whether he liked it or not. "I'll fill him in on the details before he goes home. I can arrange for us to be in Melbourne and make a start tomorrow."

"Um, right. Keep me posted on how things go. You might keep an eye open for Stewart, too, while you're in Melbourne."

"Yes, I'll be doing that."

Ron missed the warmth underlying that reply and continued, "If you find him, see if you can haul him back here. I want a piece of him!"

Q found herself thinking, 'Mm – I wonder if I do too?'

As Kaiser Ron finally managed to leave for home, Elizabeth caught Wilko's arm just as he was clearing his desk ready to also depart.

The Tasmanian looked worried. The intensity of both her grip on his arm and the look on her face did not bode well, he thought. He was right.

"Sorry sport, you're going back to Melbourne tomorrow," she told him.

"Eh? What?" the Tasmanian said, starting to lapse back into what was usually described as his goldfish impression.

"Just a little job Kaiser Ron wants done. How about I tell you about it down at the *Punters Folly*?"

"Um… I suppose so. Sure," he replied.

Wilko tried not to sound worried, but he had a definite feeling that there was trouble in store. It was just as well that he had no idea how much trouble it would be.

.oOo.

10 CROSS PURPOSES

It wasn't a dungeon, he had to admit that. No dungeon was so well furnished.

"Ah, but iron bars do not a prison make, nor stone walls a cell. Or something like that anyway," said John B., addressing an oil painting of an elderly man in a dress uniform.

The painting was one of three large pieces that adorned the walls of the room. The others were landscapes, quite possibly two different views of the same frozen lake surrounded by snow-draped trees.

The frames were opulent, and would have been more so in earlier years. The same was true of the room's furnishings. The curtains and bedcovers were lush but faded, while the bed and bedside table were beautifully crafted but scuffed and worn.

Stewart was sitting on the end of the bed, thoughtfully sipping from a cup of black tea. His flirtation with consciousness in Doctor Solo's lab had been brief. When he'd next woken properly he'd found himself in this small well-appointed bedroom. Beside his bed he'd found a pot of tea cooling and a plate of fish paste sandwiches that were only a little stale.

What had happened when he was strapped down in the lab? His memory of the experience wasn't a complete blank but it was extremely near to it.

Oddly enough it was one of the landscape paintings that was tugging at the corner of his mind. Something about the shape formed by the branches seemed dimly familiar.

The door was locked. Well, that was no real surprise. Nor was it a shock to find that there were bars on the room's only small window.

'I wonder what these buggers are doing to me? Or trying to do. I don't feel too bad now the grogginess is starting to wear off. I wonder if they'd have snatched anyone at random. Or if they picked me deliberately. Something to do with my magic maybe? Nah, that's crazy. How could they know? It's not like I walk around wearing a big pointy hat with 'Wizzard' sewn on it.'

John B. stood and paced the small distance around the room a few times, just to get some blood flowing in his legs.

He pulled the curtain aside and looked out the window. The sun was just above the trees that comprised most of his view.

"Mid-morning by the look of it," he said to himself. "Or mid-afternoon. I don't know which direction I'm facing."

With nothing else to occupy him, he quite lost track of time while watching the activities of some skinks among the foliage. Without him noticing, his eyes adapted to the fading light as gathering clouds obscured the sun. He continued to watch as heavy raindrops started to land on the foliage, the splashes adding more lustre to the metallic skin of the skinks.

There had been no sound from the door as it opened. Her footsteps were similarly soundless on the carpeted floor so the first inkling John B. had of Aleksa's entry was when he spotted her reflection in the window glass.

He'd barely begun to turn when he felt the painful jab in his arm. He fell unconscious to the floor before uttering a sound.

*

It wasn't waking up. That was too generous a description. It was more like moving into a shallower depth of unconsciousness.

All that penetrated Stewart's awareness was a faint tingling at his scalp, a distant echo of a voice, and a rhythmic metallic sound.

The rhythmic metallic sound – it was rain. Heavy rain. And hail. Falling on the roof, hammering against the windows of the grand exhibition hall.

For a moment, Stewart looked around in puzzlement, then lightning flashed and puzzlement gave way to vexation.

This storm could spoil his demonstration to the tsar. He'd waited ten years for this moment. He knew that his was not the most eye-catching display at the All-Russia Industrial and Artistic Exhibition.

Even among the scientific displays he realised the demonstration of his new discovery of what he called 'bio-electricity' lacked the obvious excitement of the first Russian automobile (capable of a frightening top speed of thirteen-and-a-half miles per hour!) or the steam-powered tractor.

Even Shukhov's hyperboloid steel tower, the first of its type anywhere in the world, outdid him for visual appeal.

But he was confident that Nikolay II would appreciate the implications of his presentation of how this unseen energy within living creatures could be demonstrated and measured. What could be measured could be harnessed, and enhanced, and *used*.

Konstantin Dashkov had used up much of the inheritance that his father the Count had left him. His wastrel older brothers may choose to fritter their money away on trifles, women, gambling and drinking, but his thirst was for knowledge.

It was his father's long-standing friendship with the tsar's family that had enabled him to secure a place here at the Nizhniy Novgorod Exhibition of 1896, amongst an array of Russia's most esteemed scientists. Mendeleyev, Timiryazev, Popov had all paid him courtesies, although only the botanist Timiryazev appeared to have any inkling of what Dashkov's researches might mean.

Thunder crashed overhead. The weather had been good ever since May. But the July storm had arrived with the tsar. As Nikolay and the Empress and the Grand Duke Aleksey Aleksandrovich made their way around the various Exhibition Halls the skies above had darkened then burst.

As Stewart, no, Dashkov – where had that odd British name come from? – stood waiting in increasing distress the sound of the weather reached a deafening crescendo.

Suddenly there was a terrible crash as the plate glass of a window somewhere above shattered with the impact of the storm. Sheeting rain poured in, soaking Dashkov and shorting out his delicate electrical measuring devices. With the rain came hailstones, some the size of walnuts. Despite Konstantin's frantic efforts to use his body as a shield, several pieces of fragile equipment were smashed.

When the royal party finally passed through, after the storm had subsided, they were sympathetic, of course. But without his meticulously constructed demonstration to support him, Dashkov's agitated words of explanation sounded at best far-fetched.

After the tsar and his entourage left the hall, Konstantin Dashkov sat disconsolately among the ruins of the expression of over a decade's work. Even the Empress' personal invitation to the royal banquet to be held in two night's time – a generous act of sympathy to the good-looking but obviously devastated young man, did not cheer him. He wasn't the partying type.

It wasn't all hopeless, of course. He still had his knowledge. He still had some of his father's money. Perhaps something might yet be discreetly done about loosening his brothers' grip on the family fortune. His musings were interrupted by a polite cough from a heavyset figure in a dark coat.

"My sympathies to you, Konstantin Dashkov," said the man. "I can only imagine your disappointment."

"Vladimir Rastorguyev, isn't it? My thanks. I shall… persevere."

"I should hope so," nodded Rastorguyev. "I saw great promise in your work."

"You are a scientist?'

The broad man shook his head and replied, "No no. I am but a humble merchant."

Dashkov looked at him penetratingly. "I know your family's name," he said. "Humble is not, I think, the word I would choose."

Vladimir smiled. "Perhaps. Certainly some of my family have, over the years, achieved some – prominence. I myself prefer to maintain a less public profile. I have noted that the heads which appear above parapets are those most likely to be shot at, one way or another."

"You mentioned seeing promise in my work."

"I see it having commercial potential. Perhaps not in and of itself, but if it may be applied to increase the yield of certain crops, or the health and vitality of certain animals…?"

The young scientist nodded, musing to himself already. "Experimentation would be expensive. And there would be those who might disapprove."

"Most especially my competitors were I suddenly to start producing significantly faster horses, more robust pigs, fatter grains. They would demand to know the secret. Your work is not yet a matter of public record, I take it?" Rastorguyev gestured around the remains of Dashkov's modest exhibit.

"No."

"Work for me, and I would ask that it remain so. Or are you one of those men motivated by fame and acclamation?"

Dashkov was silent for a few moments as he looked his potential benefactor up and down, before finally replying, "I assure you, I am not such a man. To be honest, I can give you no answer as to what motivates my work. I have rarely if ever considered that – having chanced upon my discovery I now simply pursue it. I think that it is my destiny."

"Your destiny? To be a public servant? I don't think I've ever heard it described that way!" said the surprised personnel officer behind the desk.

Dashkov shook his head. Dashkov? No, Stewart. John B. Stewart. That's what it said on the recruitment form.

"Um… sorry. Wrong word for it, I think. Fate, maybe? I think that it's what I'm meant to be doing," Stewart continued.

The personnel officer nodded, only a little less puzzled than his suddenly seemingly dazed interviewee. "Well, with a Bachelor of Arts majoring in Languages and Antiquities there's probably not a lot of career options out there for you, are you? I don't mean that nastily – I've got a B.A. in Music History gathering dust at home."

The two shared wry smiles.

The personnel officer – Mr. Luck, according to the nameplate on his desk, scanned John B.'s form again. "No interest in a teaching career?" he asked.

"None at all. I've got no desire to go back into an institution I spent years not enjoying."

"And yet your academic results were good in a broad range of subjects, and your performance in the Entrance Exam was excellent. Which is why the Department is offering you a position."

"Thanks," responded Stewart with a smile. "I didn't say I wasn't good at school, but I didn't enjoy it much either. Not at my best in a structured environment, I think."

Mr. Luck raised an eyebrow. "A word to the wise, young fella – that's not a career-enhancing comment to throw away at a recruitment interview. I'd strongly suggest you don't bring it up any time you're going for a pro-motion." He smiled again. "But I like you, and your Exam results are, as I said, excellent. Welcome to the Australian Public Service, Mr. Stewart."

The two men stood, and shook hands over Luck's desk.

"Destiny?" repeated Luck in a mix of amusement and puzzlement.

"Could mean a lot of things," replied the young man, who blinked as the world momentarily seemed to go black around him.

.oOo.

11 MEMORY TEST

It felt strange to Darren to walk into the *Punters Folly* without John B. Stewart either beside him or already sitting at the bar welcoming him.

It was a hangout for those who worked in any of the nearby Public Service departments, not usually for fast food servers, but he'd never felt unwelcome.

As he entered he waved to Wilko. They'd both shared in the events in the desert with John B., and a genuine friendship had developed. "G'day lad!" greeted Wilko and shook the young man's hand warmly. "This is Elizabeth – I don't think you've met."

Darren took the pretty brunette's hand and bowed gallantly, a gesture he'd picked up from his housemate. "We've met by phone – this morning and again this afternoon. Thanks for ringing me," he said.

Elizabeth smiled at him. "You're welcome," she said. "Have a seat."

The tall youth joined them at their table.

"You said you wanted to talk about John. Have you heard anything? Did he ring the office?" Darren's concern for his old friend was palpable.

She shook her head. "You've heard nothing either, then, obviously. When was the last time you did?"

The young man looked thoughtful then shrugged. "A few days ago. He just rang to say g'day and ask after Kat."

"How did he sound?"

"Fine. He said the work was going okay, and that he'd found a bar he liked. He was going there with you that night, Wilko."

The small man nodded. "That'd be *The Capital*. Yeah, nice place, and not too dear."

Elizabeth turned to him, a puzzled look on her face. "Hang on," she said. "I thought you said he was staying on somewhere cheaper."

"Um… cheaper accommodation I guess. Yeah, that must have been it."

Wilko shifted uncomfortably in his seat, aware that both Elizabeth and Darren were looking at him with creased brows after that innocent reply. "All of a sudden you sound a bit vague," she observed.

The Tasmanian raised his hands defensively and said, "It's been a long day at work, okay? And it finished up with you telling me I'm going back to Melbourne tomorrow to meet with these 'focus groups'. I've got a right to be a bit vague, okay?"

Darren looked surprised. "You're going back there tomorrow? Can you look out for John while you're there?"

"We will, don't worry," assured Elizabeth.

"Why all this fuss?" asked Wilko. "He's hanging around Melbourne for a few days. Going on a bender because he was feeling stressed. Maybe not his best decision ever, but he can look after himself."

"Did he sound stressed when he spoke to you, Darren?" asked the woman, her green eyes flashing.

"No. Like I said – just his normal self, and his normal self is pretty un-stressed."

"That's right," Elizabeth agreed. "And when I last spoke to him he certainly wasn't the one sounding stressed. I mean, he sounded fine. Was he behaving any differently during the project, Wilko?"

There was a silence while Wilko concentrated. There was something wrong, like a single wrong note in a complex chord.

"No, he was fine," he admitted. "Actually seemed to be enjoying the work, now I come to really think about it."

Elizabeth was dogged. "Yet at the end of the project he decides to stay there and write himself off for a while. Why would he do that?"

"His exact words were 'Nothink to worry about, all is fine.' I remember it."

"Say that again," ordered Elizabeth.

"He said 'Nothink to worry about, all is fine.'"

"Nothink?" she repeated, pronouncing the word very clearly.

"Um… yeah. That's… right." Wilko looked puzzled.

Elizabeth asked, "Since when did John sound like a '*Rocky and Bullwinkle*' villain?"

"Only when he's watching the show and reciting the lines from memory. Otherwise, not usually," Darren replied.

"Well, no. But I remember that's what he said," Wilko protested, but with more than a trace of uncertainty.

In a couple of mouthfuls Elizabeth finished the glass of wine that had been sitting on the table in front of her.

"Something is definitely not right here," she said. Resting her hand on Darren's arm she continued, "We'll be looking out for him in Melbourne, I promise."

"I thought we were going there for work?" said Wilko.

"That's not going to take all day, or all evening, for three days."

"I could go with you. Surely we can find someone to look after Kat," Darren offered.

Elizabeth shook her head and replied, "No – you'd better stay here. He might yet turn up at home, or try to get in touch with you there. I'll give you my mobile number."

"Thanks. I've got Wilko's written down by the phone at home too. I suppose that's the most sensible way to go about it. I'll ring you as soon as I hear anything. *If* I hear anything."

Wilko looked at the two others. Both wore expressions of concern. Something in his head was telling him there was nothing to be concerned about. But another voice in his head was trying to sound a warning. That one was much more like his own voice.

.oOo.

12 CROSS WORDS

The dining room had many of the same characteristics as the bedroom in which John B. had woken.

The décor spoke of faded glory. Elegant drapes and table linen had lost some of their colour, and showed small worn patches and loose threads. The timber of the dining suite and sideboard similarly showed signs of long use.

The room wasn't especially spacious, but neither was it uncomfortably cramped. Four people could be comfortably seated around the dining table, and currently were.

Even John B. was quite comfortable physically, if not at all at ease otherwise. He sat facing Aleksa, while Gleb sat with his back to the window and Dr. Solo was positioned near the only doorway out of the room.

"Eat up," the doctor encouraged his prisoner. "The potato soup is very good, I assure you."

"Made with your own fair hands?" asked Stewart wryly.

"As a matter a fact, yes. Cooking is one of the numerous skills I have mastered. I enjoy good food and long ago learned to trust only my own preparation. Present company excepted," he said, smiling to his two confederates, "But old habits die hard."

"Sensible to take precautions," agreed John B. "So you'll forgive me if I'm a little reticent about dining with people I haven't been formally introduced to."

The doctor slapped his forehead theatrically.

"Of course! How rude of me! You have not yet been in a position to be, as you say, formally introduced. The lovely Miss Yusupova you already know."

Aleksa gave a pleasant smile. The one Stewart gave in return was overtly insincere.

Dr. Solo continued. "You have, of course also encountered my other associate, albeit briefly. Comrade Gleb Venediktovich Skripitsyn. I believe he made an impression on you."

"Several," replied Stewart. "Gleb? That's a real name? I thought it must be a nickname. You know, like the sound an intelligent thought would make if it accidentally fell into the bucket of your brain."

The greasy-looking Russian glared at the wizard and growled, "I do not like you, hairy man."

"Oh, that's good!" said John B. cheerfully. "I'd hate to think my feeling for you wasn't mutual!"

"You underestimate Mr. Skripitsyn," said the doctor with a smile. "He comes from a wealthy aristocratic family. They have owned property in the province of Yaroslavl for many years."

"A well-bred ox is still an ox."

"My! Gleb did make an impression on you, didn't he? No, please sit down, Gleb. I would not like to have my dinner spoiled by a display of violence. Mr Stewart, I must tell you that my – friend, Gleb is not as stupid as he may appear to you…"

"Well, that'd be difficult. He looks like he'd need to have someone read him an instruction card on Breathing 101 at the start of every day."

"I kill…"

"Gleb! Please sit down I said! Kindly do not confirm Stewart's opinion of you by rising to his obvious baits!"

Slightly subdued by the doctor's admonishment, Skripitsyn returned to his chair. He picked up his butter knife in a way that wordlessly expressed what he'd really like to be doing with it.

Solo smiled his perfect smile at John B. and said, "He really is brighter than you give him credit for, but more importantly to me he is quite fearless and totally loyal to me. As is my dear Aleksa."

"Which brings us to you, mine host. Who are you to inspire such loyalty?"

"Tell him nothing, Doctor!" warned Gleb.

"Your sense of security does you credit, Comrade, but there is nothing to fear. Even in the remote chance Mr. Stewart could somehow escape this house, where could he go? Mr. Stewart, I am Doctor Konstantin Solovyov. Some of my - colleagues in times past took to using the epithet 'Dr. Solo'. To my surprise I found I warmed to it. I have always been inde pendently minded. I am the owner of this house and of the private island on which it rests. You are fifty miles or so from Melbourne – the water is cold and it is a long swim.”

“Not for the sharks,” observed Skripitsyn with malice.

“Duly noted, thank you,” said John B. politely. “So why are you here in this little haven of solitude? More to the point from my perspective, why am I here?”

“I am a scientist. My colleagues and I relocated here some time ago so that I could continue my research without interruption. You are a part of my research.”

“Oh – lucky me. Of course, there’s more than one kind of luck. Research, eh? Is that why I’m being fed?”

The doctor’s dazzling smile widened as he replied, “Well, we three must eat. And I feel that a good meal may relax you – make you more amenable to my procedure.”

Stewart nodded as he took a mouthful of what was, indeed, very good soup.

After swallowing he asked, “Any chance of your telling me about this procedure?”

Solovyov inclined his head. “To what end?”

“Well, it may help me feel that I’m contributing, eh?”

Aleksa laughed. “Oh but you are contributing, darlink! Contributing to the most important scientific work ever done, in Mother Russia or any where else!"

John B. couldn't suppress a wry smile. "Modesty isn't your long suit, then, Aleksa."

"The Yusupova family has a long and proud history. We have never acquired a talent for false modesty," she replied.

The doctor nodded. "Were you a student of Russian history, Mr. Stewart, you might know that it was in the palace of Prince Felix Yusupova that the rogue Rasputin met his end."

Stewart surveyed the silverware, crystal and porcelain that adorned the table before looking across at Aleksa.

"So you and Gleb are both Old Money? Yet here you are on an island at the far end of the planet, in a little wooden house, not a palace, working for Smiling Sam here. What happened?"

Aleksa replied, "There is little point in knowink which is the correct fork to eat with, when you have no food to eat with it."

"I would have thought that would be a very humbling experience. Or at least, it should have been," John B. said evenly.

The woman glared at him with a look so cold it could have frozen meat.

Some of the ice was reflected in Solovyov's smile.

"I should advise you, Mister Stewart, that it is more dangerous to antagonize Miss Yusupova than even Gleb. In a – previous occupation, she chose to extend her name in order to express more clearly her attitude to some English-speaking, er, adversaries. Aleksa Gorenya Olga Natalya

Yusupova…"

"Agony. Lovely."

"Agony Aleksa, yes, and as you say, Mr. Stewart, lovely. For quite some time now…" Dr. Solo continued, his smile directed in equal part at both Aleksa and his prisoner.

She was unmoved – a matter of long experience. "Let us be gettink on with the procedure, hah?" she suggested in a low tone.

Solovyov made a small performance out of finishing the last of his soup before answering, "I have a rather good small roast of beef awaiting carving. Still, I expect I shall be hungry after our next session. I doubt that you will be so inclined Mr. Stewart, as I propose to increase the intensity of this treatment."

John B. heard none of the last sentence, and little of the one before, as Solo had punctuated the word 'roast' by jabbing a hypodermic needle into the wizard's leg under the cover of the table and the wizard's consciousness fled quickly.

Gleb might have caught Stewart as he fell sideways from his chair to the floor. But he didn't bother.

*

This time John B. didn't even hear the sound of the machines. But the sound was there. A regular, rhythmic pounding that penetrated into the subconscious.

Pounding. Pounding. Pounding feet on a city footpath slick with Brisbane summer rain. Pounding fists, pounding into flesh just up ahead, around that corner.

"Hang on Edmund, I'm coming!"

'If you pick on my mates, you pick on me. And nobody picks on Konstan… on John B. Stewart! Must be wound up – can't even remember my own name!' The thoughts tumbled through his head in moments as he reached the alleyway from where the fight sounds were coming.

He skidded around the corner and launched himself, literally headfirst at one of the four thugs who were kicking a figure huddled on the ground.

The shaggy-haired skull slammed into the small of the thug's back. The man barely groaned as he collapsed.

The other three realized that they had company and turned their attentions to the new arrival. None of them spoke, but the nearest one swung a fist at Stewart's face. The intended target was able to dodge the blow and sank a savage kick into the would-be assailant's crotch.

As the stricken man fell forward he grabbed at the purple t-shirt, pulling Stewart off balance.

The other two attackers saw their opportunity and advanced on him.

Stewart felt curiously detached, as if he was watching the events unfold from a distance.

In a split second the events of the past few minutes flashed across his mind.

Drinks with his University mates Bruce Bond and Edmund Mapleton in a city bar. Bruce had left early to pick up his younger brother Darren. Then Edmund decided he'd had enough and was ready to leave. Stewart went to the men's room after promising to meet Edmund outside. When he got to the footpath, there was no sign of his friend.

Asking the bouncer at the hotel door if he'd seen anything elicited only a grunt in reply. Then a couple leaving the bar, hearing the exchange, had said in worried tones that they'd 'seen the big guy being followed out here and hassled by four blokes'.

Edmund was a big guy, but after an accident had done terrible damage to his knees, he walked with difficulty. He was a much easier target than he looked for boys who wanted to look tough.

Faced with the couple's news the bouncer grunted again and said, "What happens outside ain't any of my concern," before looking away.

A drunk had looked up from vomiting in the gutter and croaked, "Went tha' way."

Stewart had run in the direction the drunk had indicated, towards a dark alleyway between two of the city's surviving old buildings.

It was the dark alleyway in which the two youths were now about to attack him. Not a wise move, had they known, for Stewart was neither sober nor calm and that was a volatile combination.

The heavier thug lunged first, grabbing Stewart's arms to pinion him.

Momentum carried them back a few paces until a wall brought them up short.

"Now we got ya," growled the taller, leaner youth as he moved to follow them and go for Stewart's eyes and throat.

But suddenly he crashed to the ground. The battered Edmund had reached out, grabbed the thug's ankles and yanked. It wasn't a graceful landing.

Stewart seized the moment and pushed off from the wall, twisting out of the clumsy grip he was held in. His beefy assailant tripped over his own mate and fell backwards awkwardly. The tall one went to get up but his last conscious sight for a while was Stewart's left boot on a rapid collision course with his face.

The remaining stocky youth again struggled to his feet and again tried to lunge at Stewart. His reward was a right cross that did some damage to his jaw, a head butt that stunned him, and as he fell a vicious knee that cracked ribs.

Edmund by now had also managed to struggle to his feet. He looked around at the damage, relieved but also more than a little shocked.

He opened his mouth to say something but Stewart laid a finger on his lips and shook his head.

The shaggy figure squatted down beside the first thug he'd felled – the one most conscious – and said, very clearly and distinctly, "This is what you get when you mess with the Blades."

Edmund looked at Stewart strangely, then the penny dropped. There was known to be a small 'turf war' going on amongst Brisbane's city gangs. Stewart had ensured that in the unlikely event that the four thugs complained to the police (or the more likely event that they were asked awkward questions by a doctor) the blame would be directed at one of the better known and less popular active gangs. If he'd just inflamed the 'turf war' a little further, that might be considered a happy bonus if it took off the streets a few more of the individuals whose idea of a good time was a mugging.

Stewart propped himself under Mapleton's arm for support and in a much quieter voice said, "Looks like your ribs copped a real kicking. We better get you to a hospital, brother."

"Ah, a hospital – it will do me no good, my brother," said Vladimir Dash-kov, shaking his head. "The infirmary here in the abbey is as good a place as any in which to die."

Konstantin shrugged. "As you wish. It is where you have chosen to live."

His brother – the second of the three – sighed. "You have not called me 'brother' for a long time, Kosta. And I have not deserved it. You no longer even call yourself a Dashkov. Have Mikhail and I so tarnished the family name?"

Again the younger man shrugged. "I am a pragmatic man. I now choose to be John… *nyevyehrnah* - Konstantin Tretyakov because, unlike others,

I see our country's future. The aristocracy is dying, both its power and its prestige. Now is the time to be a part of the merchantry."

"They too are dying, as this 'Blue Death' sweeps our country," said Vladimir sadly. "It spares none – young or old, pious or profane, poor or rich. Even here in this abbey, where we had thought ourselves protected by the hand of the Divine..."

His voice trailed off sadly.

'Cloistering yourself from the ills that your 'flock' must face,' was the thought that flitted through the younger brother's mind, rapidly followed by the contented recollection of how cholera had been brought to his brother's refuge.

One application of his work with bioelectricity had been to dramatically increase Vladimir Rastorguyev's pig stock's resistance to disease. To test some of his work Konstantin had obtained a sample of a particularly aggressive strain of cholera.

He had been quietly delighted to find that his 'enhanced' hogs were not succumbing to the disease after exposure. He had then wanted to test the efficacy of the enhancement process on himself, but needed a 'control subject' whose biology and genetic profile closely matched his own.

Eldest brother Mikhail was inconveniently distant on some military exercise, so Konstantin had got in touch with his middle sibling. As the second son, Vladimir had joined the clergy as family tradition dictated. Priestly robes had not, however, covered either his avaricious nature or his carnal appetites.

His capacity for food and alcohol had made Vladimir a florid and corpulent man who had already looked much older than his years. His depletion of his share of the Dashkov estate, rapid during his seminary days, had slowed when he could supplement his income with the ruthlessly and/or cunningly extracted tithes and 'donations' from his parishioners.

Soon after Konstantin's first visit to his brother in many years those parishioners started to fall victim to the plague that was creeping across Russia, and the priestly Dashkov had fled to the sanctuary of a nearby abbey. There, at least, sanitation was better and they had their own supply of clean drinking water.

When subsequently visiting the abbey, continuing the charade of re-establishing filial affection, it had been an easy task for the newly renamed K. Tretyakov to add a small but highly contaminated sample of water to his brother's wine. It had been a very non-Communion French red, Konstantin recalled.

He looked down at his stricken brother on the bare straw pallet, satisfied that here was proof that his own 'enhancement' was working. The fluid loss from the violent diarrhea and vomiting had given Vladimir's features the grey pallor that gave the 'Blue Death' its name. Already the skin, stretched by fat, was starting to hang in obvious folds.

Vladimir closed his sunken eyes as he labored to draw breath. "I have tried... to contact Mikhail but he is... too busy... playing soldiers to come to me in my… hour of need."

The eyelids flickered open again as the dying man gazed up at his brother and continued, "I must of course make an appropriate… disbursement to… Mother Church, but… most of what I have… has been left to you, Kosta. With my… gratitude for your… being here…"

The dry voice faded to little more than a gasp.

The youngest brother bowed his blonde head in a gesture of acknowledgment, if not gratitude or even respect.

'It is as it should be,' he thought to himself, and regarded what would soon be his brother's corpse distastefully. 'I wish never to look so… so… unappealing.'

The ashen face suddenly grew hazy. Konstantin Tretyakov closed his eyes and steadied himself.

Konstantin Solovyov opened his eyes and drew a deep, steadying breath.

So did John B. Stewart.

.o0o.

13 PLANE SPEAKING

One way of recognizing people who do a lot of domestic air travel is to watch them eat.

Even in an expensive restaurant or at a large dining table, while handling their cutlery they habitually keep their elbows tucked in tightly against their ribs, using forearms and wrists at an angle reminiscent of a preying mantis.

It's because they've become so used to trying to feed themselves in a narrow space, where a stray elbow from or into the person beside you could result in a forkful of fish casserole being rammed up your nostril.

On the crowded morning flight to Melbourne, Q and Wilko were readying themselves for just that posture as breakfast was served.

Q peeled the lid off her foil tray and started to tuck in. Wilko looked at the offering she'd opened. A yellow cube of something purported to be an omelet quivered in a corner of the tray, apparently trying to hide behind a green mound of wilted spinach. Q's plastic fork chased a fragment of hard skinny sausage around in a little puddle of grease.

A lover of good food, Wilko sighed and put down his unopened packet of plastic cutlery.

"I think I'll just have the orange juice," he said quietly.

"In a couple of weeks I'll probably agree with you," his travelling companion replied, "I'm afraid that right now any meal I don't have to cook myself is a good one."

Wilko looked at her quizzically.

Without looking up from her tray she quietly explained, "I've been chief cook and bottle-washer for Sonny for years. The only time he's ever worked in the kitchen was to paint it five years ago. Now there's just me in my own unit at least I've only got my own tastes to please but I'm still the only hand in the kitchen."

The Tasmanian considered this for a while. Kaiser Ron had been the only person in whom Q had confided, and that only because she'd needed the day off to move. Uncharacteristically, the boss had managed to resist feeding the office rumour mill with the news.

Cautiously Wilko began, "So you and Sonny are…?"

"Me and Sonny aren't. And yes, I'm happier for it. It's been a long time coming."

"As long as you're okay," he replied sincerely.

Q looked up from her breakfast and smiled. "Yeah. It'll take a bit of adjusting, but I'm okay. Thanks."

Wilko returned the smile. He sat silently for a while, reading the financial pages of the newspaper. In a moment of weakness while driving back from Central Australia he'd bought a parcel of cheap shares in a fledgling opal mining operation. Now he wasn't surprised to see that their value had scarcely moved. In reality he was more concerned with digesting the unexpected news of the Dances' separation.

Meanwhile Q finished eating, and sat gazing out the aircraft window while trying to digest the egg, spinach, and whatever the sausage had been made of.

The pilot announced the commencement of what would be a slow descent into Melbourne.

Wilko turned to his companion and asked, "Elizabeth – please tell me why we're coming to Melbourne."

"Because Ron can't safely sign off the testing of the project until we've properly evaluated the user reactions. Because he's realized I'm the best person he's got to ask the right questions and get the right answers. Because I need you to answer any technical questions the users might come up with," she replied, marking off each 'because' on her fingers.

"Uh-huh. That all makes sense. And is there anything else?"

"I want to find John. I can't help feeling there's something wrong," she admitted.

Given the earlier revelation, Wilko tried to sound diplomatic as he asked, "Are you and John… er… an item, as they say?"

There was no hint of deception and no break in eye contact as Q evenly replied, "No. We're just friends. But right now friends are more important to me than ever. I don't have a family I can turn to."

Wilko looked concerned. He was very close to his own family, and couldn't imagine facing a time of crisis without their support.

Elizabeth continued. "I know you said John told you not to worry, and I'm not accusing you or blaming you for anything, but I've got an instinct that he's in trouble. You were there with him, you might have a better idea of where to start looking."

"Well okay – we can try. If we can't unearth him in a few days, and he hasn't called Darren or Kaiser Ron by then, we can go see the police. Of course, he could be in a cell somewhere already, drying out. That's happened before, I think."

"Maybe. A long time ago. Wherever he is now, I can't shake the idea that it's not anywhere that he wants to be."

.oOo.

"It was never – *ugh* – my intention to be – *aargh* – a domestic servant!" Gleb grunted as he dropped a load of freshly chopped wood into a basket beside the fireplace.

"Are you feelink your age, comrade?" purred Aleksa as she replaced the crystal glasses she'd been cleaning to their place on the mantlepiece. "I am younger than you, Aleksa Gorenya!" snapped the burly man.

She smiled and shrugged. "To us, what does it matter? Some domestic chores are a small price to pay to live in somethink like the manner to which we were accustomed."

She waved a manicured hand to indicate the surrounding room. "*Da*, we have less space than we used to, but the situation is more than adequate, the climate is reasonably kind. It is only a little warmer than what we left behind."

"We obtain – others, as we require them. Why not obtain some servants? They are expendable."

Aleksa smiled at Gleb's suggestion. She'd heard it before. "This is not the old country. Here there can be… consequences if people are missed. You know that. It is why we must be so careful in acquiring those others of whom you speak."

Gleb grunted as he unenthusiastically pushed a broom across the timber floorboards visible around the faded Turkish rug that centred the room. It was his normal response when he was unhappy, which was his usual state of mind. This natural belligerence was one of the characteristics that had made him so useful to Dr. Solo for so long.

Aleksa continued, "The doctor and I maintain the facility downstairs. That in turn maintains us. Is it so much to ask that you and I keep up here habitable?"

The reply was another grunt before Gleb turned to glare at her. "You asked am I feeling my age. Yes, Comrade Aleksa, I am. You and the doctor promised much of this dog we are keeping in there," he said, jerking a meaty thumb towards Stewart's room. "Enough for all of us, you said. And yet, after three attempts at the procedure even Solo himself has nothing to show for it. I say he is a mistake and we should feed him to the sharks."

Dr. Solo stepped out from his own bedroom. He had been standing silently in the doorway, unnoticed by either of his minions.

He smiled his immaculate smile, but there was no warmth behind it. "Dear Gleb," he said smoothly, "I respect your passion, but even now you have not learned patience."

If the doctor shared the ugly man's concerns he gave no indication of it. He smoothed down the lapels of the smoking jacket he wore.

"Aleksa," he called. "A small sedative for Mr. Stewart, please. To borrow a local phrase, let us have another go."

Yusupova restrained a reflexive flinch. To hear the characteristically for mal Solovyov slip into Australian vernacular was disconcerting. Instead she offered a small nod.

"As you say, Doctor," she replied. "The – patient – will be ready for Gleb to convey to the laboratory very shortly."

"Splendid," said Solo. "I shall prepare the machines."

*

Solovyov sat comfortably in his usual chair. Stewart lay in a twilight sleep on the table. Both had their usual array of wires attached.

At the doctor's bidding, Aleksa had changed some of the settings on her control panel. It was hoped this might improve the effectiveness of the procedure. Solo was confident that there was no risk, and had no qualms about any risk to the man strapped down opposite him.

The machines that lined the downstairs laboratory beat out their usual rhythm. It was a regular pounding, like the beat of a mechanical pulse.

The mechanical pulse still beat in the food processing factory, but less strongly than Vladimir Rastorguyev would have preferred.

Sitting in his office, strategically overlooking much of the key work, he gave a worried smile to the man whose scientific genius had allowed his business to survive where others had fallen under the pressure of govern-ment expectations and regulations.

"I confess that I do find it – almost distasteful, that we owe our continued existence to this conflict with Japan. I do not like war, for all that it does not seem to trouble you, Konstantin."

Tretyakov blinked for a moment, as if he hadn't recognised his name, then shrugged.

"I am a practical man, Vladimir. This war gave us – you – a valuable contract to supply rations to our troops. A contract we won on merit. The meat which comes from this factory is superior to any produced in the country."

The businessman nodded and said, "Yes, yes. Due in no small part to you. But the death and destruction… I fear this war ages me, as if I needed that! You seem to be suffering no such ill-effects at least. It seemed like such an opportunity for glory for our country. Certainly that is what our government sold the promise of."

"And to be fair, Vladimir, in those first days that promise seemed destined to be fulfilled. And we, at least, go on. Take comfort, if you will, from the fact that we help ensure that our soldiers are fed." He smiled. "We cannot make them indestructible."

Rastorguyev got up from his leather chair with a sigh, and paced slowly over to the window that afforded him his view over the factory floor. "Perhaps I might wish that there was something in your research that could. Your brother may still be alive, eh?"

Tretyakov's smile disappeared. "Mikhail was a fool," he snapped. "A wastrel and a fool unworthy of such advantages as his family name had furnished him. He joined the army and became an officer because it was expected of him. He volunteered to take so *prominent* a role in this war because the promotion meant better pay. And because he had heard of my involvement in the contract your firm won. I fancy he imagined that he might somehow turn that to his own financial advantage.”

The businessman shook his head sadly. There was no doubting the genius of Dashkov, or Tretyakov as he now styled himself, but the man seemed to have a total lack of compassion.

“I cannot imagine where such an idea could have come from. The nature of your work here is a well kept secret.”

“But it is known that I am now a partner in the business. The government demands to know such things. Evidently someone revealed my identity to the greedy idiot Mikhail.”

The scientist was not about to mention to his business partner, or anyone else, that he had been the one who had passed the confidential information to the “greedy idiot”. He had known that his eldest sibling would be open to the suggestion that there might be a profit to be turned from the war for a man in ‘just the right place’.

“Was life with your brother so terrible when you were young, Konstantin?” asked Vladimir.

“I recall having little to do with either of my brothers. I was left to study while they were groomed for their roles in society, and to eventually take over the estate.”

"An estate you now possess, my friend. Have you no wish to reclaim the title of Count Dashkov?"

The scientist leaned back in his own comfortable leather chair and asked in return, "To what end? Titles are meaningless. I will inherit whatever is left of the estate itself after Mikhail's debts are paid – debts to vodka houses, prostitutes and gambling dens. There may yet be some value there. That is the sole importance of the past to me, friend Vladimir – whatever I may extract from it."

Somewhat irked by the well-intentioned reflections on his own history, Tretyakov frowned as he gazed into the lights that illuminated the factory's busy workings.

He gazed into the lights. He gazed into the lights, blinking as they momentarily wavered out of focus.

The traffic light was red. That lone oncoming car would be stopping, so even without a 'Walk' sign in his favour it would be safe to trot across the road.

He wanted to meet a particular young lady when she finished her late shift at midnight, and he only had a few minutes to get to the door of the building where she worked.

John B. jogged out onto the road, then realised with a shock that the car was accelerating, not slowing down. He broke into a sprint just in time. As the car sped past behind him he called over his shoulder, "Hey! That was a red light, you dill!"

He'd only just reduced the sprint back down to a jog as he reached the opposite footpath when he heard a squeal of tyres.

Reflected in a shop window he saw the car that had just missed him doing a screeching turn. It was his turn to almost run into the car as it slewed to a halt partially mounting the footpath in front of him.

Stewart barely had time to register what was happening, far less wonder about it, when the rear doors of the car were flung open. Two large men in blue shirts jumped from the vehicle. They grabbed him by the arms, picked him up and flung him into the back of the car.

Stunned more by the suddenness of the assault than its force he was still able to register two more figures in the car – another blue-shirted man who was obviously the driver, and an older man wearing a coat in the front passenger seat.

The two assailants quickly clambered back into the car and slammed their doors shut.

John B. hadn't been at University long, but he knew enough to realise where he was – in an unmarked police car.

"What - ?" was all he managed to get out before one of the blue-shirted men thumped a fist into his stomach, winding him.

More blows came as the car took a winding route through the city.

Eventually Stewart got a little bit of breath back. "Where -?" he began.

The older man turned and leaned back over the front seat, then landed a ferocious back-handed slap across John B.'s face. The young man felt the blood start to trickle, and realised that the man was wearing an ornate ring which had opened a deep wound.

He tried to let his body go limp to better absorb the blows. 'No way to fight back or even defend myself. Better stay quiet and hope I live through this,' he thought.

The circuitous drive brought them eventually to the city watch-house. He was bundled out of the car and into a cell. The two other occupants of the Spartan room, both of whom were seriously drunk judging by the smell, had passed out on the floor. John B. hoped they were only asleep as he slumped onto the small hard bench seat.

The duty officer in the watch-house addressed him through the bars, "What's the charge gonna be?"

"Um… pardon?" said Stewart, puzzled by the question.

"Well, it could be public drunkenness, or offensive language – what's yer pick?"

Stewart was probably in shock, but this made no sense to him.

Baffled, he replied, "I haven't had a drink since yesterday, and I didn't swear at anyone. All I said was, 'That was a red light, you dill' when the car nearly ran over me."

A voice came from beyond his line of sight outside the cell, saying, "I distinctly heard the hairy bastard f***ing swear, didn't you Sergeant?"

Another voice replied, "Yes sir, Detective Inspector O'Shaughnessy, too f***ing right."

O'Shaughnessy – the man who'd been in the front passenger seat of the unmarked car, the man with the ornate ring - stepped into view. He wrinkled his nose and gave the duty officer a sneering grin.

"Take a whiff of this cell. Obvious he's drunk, eh?"

"Yes sir, Detective Inspector," came the reply from the other man a pace behind the detective. John B. now recognised the bloke as the driver of the unmarked car.

Stewart slumped on the seat. D. I. O'Shaughnessy was well known – a high profile police spokesman when it came to being Tough on Crime, particularly civil disobedience. He was known to have a special dislike of students. The popular theory was that this was because he hadn't been able to get into University like his brother the lawyer.

John B. knew perfectly well that no judge was going to take the word of a scruffy Arts student over the media face of law enforcement. The D. I. laughed and threw an arm round the shoulders of his driver.

"Let's go, Dave," he said. "Constable, he's all yours," he told the watch-house officer as they departed back into the night.

The duty officer allowed himself a small sigh, now that he wasn't under the gaze of O'Shaughnessy himself.

"So, like I said, what's the charge gonna be?" he said.

John B. didn't look up. "What's the difference?"

"The size of the fine, or the length of the sentence if you can't pay it," explained the policeman, with something like a note of apology in his voice.

"I'll take the cheaper option, thanks," Stewart replied dispiritedly, and signed the appropriate paperwork that was passed through the bars to him.

So it was that John B. officially went onto police files as a drunk. When he was released the next morning after the routine eight hours in the watch-house he set about starting to live up to the charge. He hadn't even bothered to clean the blood off his face when he threw down the first whisky, cursing D. I. O'Shaughnessy in particular and policemen in general.

The scar left by the ring would not be the only scar he would long carry from that night.

As Aleksa disconnected the skullcap and removed it from his head, the doctor scowled. He was barely refreshed by the treatment, and found himself returning to consciousness unaccountably angry. It took several seconds of deep breathing for the feeling to be dispelled.

.o0o.

15 THE MAN WHO WASN'T THERE

The first 'focus group' sessions had gone quite well. The participants genuinely appreciated being asked for their opinions. It was something of a novelty to at least feel that they could contribute something to the running of their own jobs. The more usual management approach was for new policies, systems and procedures to be devised and imposed by people who would never be at the pointy end of their implementation.

Elizabeth was, as she'd confidently told Ron, a very effective facilitator. She got honest answers from people, but carefully promoted positive attitudes and responses.

Wilko had little to do but sit and admire her work. He modestly acknowledged some kind words about how helpful he and Stewart had been during the testing.

"How is John? Couldn't the department afford to send him too?" asked one of the group light-heartedly.

Wilko answered uncertainly, saying, "He's still in Melbourne, actually. He needed some time off. Stress leave."

"Really? He didn't seem the type to be stressed!"

There was genuine surprise and concern amongst the staff. That wasn't lost on Elizabeth who looked sidelong at her Tasmanian friend.

"So none of you have seen him around?" she asked casually.

No one had, not that any of them had expected to bump into him in their regular haunts.

As soon as the consultation session was over and the group disbanded, Elizabeth grabbed Wilko's arm.

"Your idea about going to the police – I think it's a good one," she said.

"Hang on a minute. I thought we were going to wait for a few days. Look around and see if he turns up under his own steam."

Elizabeth frowned. "Well, yes… But you heard them – nobody had any idea John was feeling *stressed*." She poured sarcasm into the word. "Neither did you, right?"

Wilko raised his hands helplessly. "I told you what he said."

"And you told me how he said it. There's something not right I'm telling you, but no, I guess we don't have much to give them. Okay – let's start on our looking around. You were both staying at the Regal, weren't you? I saw the dockets when they came into Kaiser Ron's office. I'd have booked a couple of rooms there for us, but they're full."

The Tasmanian nodded. "Yeah. The Regal's a nice place, but it's not cheap. Without the department paying for the room, I can understand why he'd want to move somewhere cheaper!"

"We've got to start somewhere, mate. Lead the way."

*

The visit to the Regal added considerably to the mystery, to Wilko's confusion, and to Q's concern.

Not only was John B. not there, but according to the girl at the reception desk he'd technically never actually left.

The cleaner had been sent into Mr. Stewart's room, with him expected to have checked out at the same time as Mr. Wilkes. She had been surprised to find all of his clothes and possessions still there.

Q insisted that the hotel manager be called to the desk. Leo Cappello was his name, and under Elizabeth's withering glare he did his best to be helpful but there was little he could offer.

Mr. Stewart had not formally checked out of the hotel. He hadn't returned the card that opened the door to his room, but the coding on the magnetic stripe that operated the lock would have expired anyway, so the Regal wasn't concerned about hotel security.

"What about your customer's security?" Elizabeth snapped.

Leo squirmed. "Well, ah… the account was paid…"

"I know! I'm the one who authorized the payment!"

"It's only been a couple of days. It sometimes happens that guests make… ah… other arrangements for a night or two…"

"Without taking their clothes?" she asked acidly.

Cappello bit down hard on a reply to the effect that for some of the 'other arrangements' a lack of clothes was almost prerequisite. Instead he settled for saying, "Not usually."

Wilko contributed a question as his own concerns started to grow. "You haven't heard anything from him? No messages?"

"Nothing at all, Mr. Wilkes, I'm sorry."

Elizabeth's voice was quiet as she asked, "There were no – signs of violence, were there?"

The manager looked concerned as he tried to remember the maid's report. Eventually he replied, "It was not tidy, I think. But we do not require that of our guests. Truthfully, we seldom even expect it. There were some clothes scattered on the floor and perhaps on the bed. Magazines were left on the desk. Nothing unusual. All of the property is now being securely held, of course."

"Of course. We'll collect that later," advised Elizabeth.

"But if Mr. Stewart comes to collect it…?"

"If Mr. Stewart comes to collect his stuff you make sure he knows we've got it," she replied, handing Leo her departmental business card. "There are people in Canberra who know how to reach us. If he turns up here without getting in touch with any of them I'll be surprised. And so will he!"

.oOo.

16 PROBING QUESTIONS

"Do you remember anything of your experiences in the treatment room?" asked Solovyov politely.

"Treatment room? Is that what you call your Frankenstein's laboratory? What is there to remember? You or the lovely Aleksa use me as a pincushion again, I find myself strapped to a steel table – a blanket would be nice by the way – you're sitting watching me. I think we both look like electric rabbis if the thing on my head looks like yours. My head feels like it's been in a spin dryer, then I either wake up in your guest room or slung over Gleb's shoulder on my way there. Are those clear enough recollections for you?"

The doctor smiled. "If it is of any comfort to you, I too am struggling to recall more than faint impressions."

"No comfort at all, really," said John B.

The doctor and his 'subject' were alone in the small parlour, seated in comfortable chairs that were upholstered with red velvet. Or what must originally been red velvet – it was now more like a dark pink.

"I wish I could get out of here," said John B. evenly.

"But of course you can! Getting out of here is simplicity itself. With the condition that getting out alive is not, I'm afraid, an option." Solo smiled his perfect smile.

Stewart didn't return the expression. His face was studiedly blank as he replied, "Don't bet on that."

The smile didn't falter. "I am not a betting man," said the doctor.

Stewart's expression changed to one of puzzlement. "I think… I've heard that before," he said after a moment of perplexity.

Perhaps for a moment a similar shadow crossed Solovyev's face, but if so he shook it off immediately.

"You remain admirably calm and courteous, Mr. Stewart. I am impressed."

"No point in losing my temper when there's nothing to be gained by it. Anger can be useful sometimes, but I've got a feeling this isn't one of them."

Solo nodded. "Wise. But I can sense your hostility, nonetheless."

"Well, what else can you expect under the circumstances?"

"Indeed. I would doubtless chafe in your position. I think we are quite similar in some ways."

"You reckon? I don't recall holding anyone prisoner while I stuck wires in their head!"

Solovyev chuckled in response. "Perhaps not. And yet I sense that like me, you are a man who rankles under authority. A non-conformist. An unlikely man to hold a government job."

"Mm. You're not the first to make that observation, although it usually comes from people who've known me longer," observed John B. wryly.

"I think I know you… surprisingly well, Mr. Stewart."

"That might just be mutual. For instance, I reckon you're not much of a one for working inside the system either. Although I also reckon you have."

The doctor nodded. "Granted, yes. As I said, we are not unalike."

"You never did tell me what your 'procedure' is supposed to achieve," said Stewart casually, perhaps hoping to catch Solo off-guard.

If it worked, there was no indication of it. The Russian shrugged and said, "There seems little point, I'm afraid. Once it has succeeded you will know nothing of it anyway."

"Is that what this is about? Memory theft? What's the point? I'm just an ordinary bloke," John B. said. 'Other than somehow making magic happen, that is,' he thought to himself.

Solovyev raised his eyebrows. "Memory theft? No. That is an interesting side effect, I do admit. One that in – earlier times, I might have been prevailed upon to explore much further. But as you rightly observed I do not work 'inside a system'. My objectives are my own. And let me say, you are most certainly not an ordinary man. Your blood test results are extraordinary."

"I really doubt that. I've had blood tests done before – I reckon my doctor would have noticed if there was anything extraordinary about me."

Dr. Solo smiled again and shook his golden head. "I don't think so," he replied. "Nobody does blood tests like I do."

He rested a genial hand on the leg of John B., who barely managed to avoid flinching.

"You may rest, my friend. You have put up remarkable resistance but your powers have their limits. My machines do not. I will instruct Aleksa to make further adjustments."

"You have a lot of faith in her, don't you?"

Again the doctor shrugged and said, "She has developed an affinity for my machines. She feels a much closer regard for the equipment than for most people, I think."

John B. thought back to the bar of *The Capital*, reflecting on the consequences of chatting with Agony Aleksa.

"Well, I do wish that closeness reaps the reward it deserves," he said.

"Oh it does!" replied Dr. Solovyev blithely.

.oOo.

17 HE WASN'T THERE AGAIN TODAY

It had been another productive day in Melbourne for Q and Wilko. Provided your definition of 'productive' coincided with Kaiser Ron's, that is.

There had been more focus groups that had produced positive results for the project. Any technical questions had been briskly and confidently dealt with by Wilko, who found himself warming to the role of 'expert'.

But those groups had also continued to echo the sentiment that John B. Stewart 'didn't seem to have been stressed'.

Over lunch, the Canberra pair had visited *The Capital*. No sooner had they entered when the barman greeted Wilko.

"Welcome back, mate!" he said cheerfully. "I thought you were heading back to Canberra?"

"Well, yeah, I did, but I had to come back," replied the Tasmanian.

The barman smiled at Elizabeth and said, "With new company, I see. Welcome to the *Capital*, ma'am. The other bloke – your mate in the purple, he didn't come back with you, then? Not something I said, I hope."

He chuckled at what he thought was a harmless remark. Q's answering smile was thin.

"Actually, we thought he was still here. You haven't seen him, then?" she said.

The barman looked a little puzzled. "Er… no, not since you were both here." He directed his answer at Wilko, shifting a little uncomfortably under the brunette's polite but unwavering gaze.

Attempting to be helpful under the green-eyed stare he suggested, "You might ask Phil when he comes on shift this afternoon – maybe he's seen him? Now, can I – er – get you both a drink, and order some lunch?"

They'd had lunch and returned to the office, where the afternoon passed just as the morning had. The focus groups went well, although an astute observer might have spotted that Elizabeth Dance was herself a little less focused than she could have been. Wilko was not that astute observer – he too was similarly distracted by the growing sense that something wasn't right.

Their afternoon assessment of the day's work was perfunctory, although neither of them openly spoke of wanting to dash back to *The Capital* to talk to Phil.

There was no clear reason to expect that the evening shift barman would provide any clues. But both of them, even Wilko who was ordinarily utterly unimaginative, were anxious. Both had a sense that there was something to be learned.

While they waited for the shift to change they sat at the bar, slowly consuming their drinks, each apparently lost in thought.

Abruptly Elizabeth asked, "Have you ever looked into John's eyes?"

"What sort of question is that?" sputtered Wilko in some indignation.

"Oh, I don't mean romantically, you dill. Just – *looked* at his eyes.
There's something – I don't know – a bit special about them."

"Is bloodshot special?"

Elizabeth pursed her lips. "Not what I meant and you know it. No, no
it's like, his eyes are older than he is. Do you understand? Have you
noticed it?"

"Nope. And nope," replied the straightforward son of Tasmania. He
frowned at his companion. "You're not taking this 'magic' nonsense of
his seriously, are you?"

His frown only deepened when she didn't laugh in response. Instead she
said, "I'm not so sure about that."

"Well, it would be nice if he'd left a trail of magic pixie dust so we could
find him!" was the grumpy reply.

The brunette smiled at that.

"You sure he hasn't cast a spell on you?" asked Wilko, venturing to tease
cautiously.

"Hah! I'm not the type, mate! We're just good friends, that's all."

Wisely Wilko let the matter drop. They nursed their drinks and waited
for the late shift staff to arrive.

They got lucky. The bar had emptied of the other afternoon patrons when
the new shift arrived so they were able to get the evening man's undivided
attention for a little while. Phil was a little nonplussed by the intensity of
the questioning he got from Elizabeth, but he'd been in the job for a long

time.

"The last time I saw him was definitely last week," he said. "He was with that blonde – the same one you were drinking with the next evening."

Wilko looked puzzled.

"Me? When was this?" he asked.

Phil looked at the two of them. Their body language certainly gave no indication that they were a couple, so he decided that Wilko wasn't being evasive on the woman's behalf. It did seem an odd question though.

"The last time you were here. Friday, wasn't it? Remember - the foreign woman?"

Wilko shook his head blankly. "I've got no idea what you're talking about. Friday I was at work. John… John didn't show up, so after work I… I…"

Elizabeth stared hard at him. She could almost hear the wheels going around in his head as he struggled to remember.

"I… came down here to look for him, I think?"

"Is that when you had the conversation about him staying on in Melbourne?" she asked.

The Tasmanian shrugged. "I guess it must have been, though I – um – don't actually remember any detail, come to think of it."

Phil shook his head. "No mate, sorry. I remember you asking me about him then. You were on your own, right up till the time the blonde came and joined you."

"What blonde is this?" asked Elizabeth.

"She comes in here, not often, but not uncommon either," explained the barman. "She was chatting to your mate when he was on his own a couple of times, then she chatted you last time you came in."

"Why can't I remember that? I think I know the woman who you're talking about though. Didn't she sit over there? I remember she had a very flash mobile phone she was using."

Phil nodded. "That's the one. Come to think of it, she was with your pal in the purple shirt last time I saw him. Might even have left together, though I couldn't swear to that."

Elizabeth's voice was cold enough to chill several of Phil's excellent martinis as she asked, "What do you know about her?"

The barman wasn't going to mess with the owner of that voice, and determined to be as helpful as possible.

He replied, "Not much. Like I said, she's only in here occasionally. Usually sits in the same place, usually texting or whatever she does on that fancy phone or whatever it is. Foreign accent – Eastern European I think."

"As in – 'nothink to worry about' maybe?" suggested his green eyed inquisitor.

Phil grinned a little and said, "Hey that's pretty good. Yeah – that's about what she sounds like. Her and the big ugly guy that usually comes in at the same time have got the same accent. I reckon they know each other but they never sit together. Not that I blame her!"

Elizabeth raised a questioning eyebrow.

"I shouldn't say this about a customer, but seriously, if I had a dog that ugly I'd shave his bum and teach him to walk backwards. You'd never say it in earshot of him of course – he's a *big* bloke!"

"I reckon I remember seeing him, too," admitted Wilko.

"Anything else you know about them?" asked the brunette.

Phil shrugged. "They come in sometimes. They sit at different tables and have a couple of drinks, usually vodka, then leave. Sometimes I'll see her chat to a bloke at the bar, usually an out of towner, not one of the regulars. I did wonder if she was, you know, a working girl. We don't get them in here as a rule. The big bloke would be a scary enough pimp! But I've never seen any evidence of it and you know, she just didn't really seem the type. You really don't remember talking to her last week?"

Wilko shook his head. "Total blank," he said.

They ordered drinks and let Phil get on with serving the other customers who had started coming in.

"This is getting seriously weird," observed Q.

"Why can't I remember what happened last Friday?" complained Wilko, as much to himself as to his companion.

"That's what I'd like to know, amongst other things," was her reply.

"You're not usually this vague."

"Thanks. I think."

"I'm going to ask around – see if anyone else here knows anything about

Madame Natasha or whatever her name is."

Elizabeth's enquiries drew a blank. A couple of the regulars recognised the description of either or both of the characters she was asking about, but knew nothing more about them than Phil.

"Come on, drink up," she instructed Wilko. "If they drink here, they might eat or shop or even live nearby. Let's go ask around."

The Tasmanian by now knew better than to argue. He finished his beer then trailed out of the *Capital* behind Elizabeth, still bemused by the hole in his memory and deeply concerned that it was the key to his old friend's disappearance.

*

They'd visited shops, cafes, restaurants and bars in a little over a block either side of *The Capital* when Q spotted something across the road.

"That might be worth a look," she said, pointing.

It was a small shop, wedged between a bakery and a photographic store. The sign over the door was in Cyrillic script, but underneath in English were the words *Balkan Supermarket*.

They crossed the road briskly and went inside.

The shop was small, barely wider than its own doorway. It was packed with shelves full of bottles, jars, tins and packets most of which were labeled incomprehensibly to Wilko and Q. Csabai sausages and other smallgoods hung from the ceiling.

Behind the counter stood a petite young dark haired woman. Behind her sat a grey bearded man who was probably not as old as he looked, apparently engrossed in reading a history textbook. They both looked up in mild surprise at the entry of two people who weren't regular customers.

To the considerable relief of Elizabeth and Wilko the pair turned out to speak English – the girl passably, the man impeccably. To their even greater relief, they were able to provide the first glimmer of light on the two 'Eastern Europeans'.

"*Da*, I know who you mean," the girl said. "They shop here quite regular. Sometime vun, sometime other."

"We'd have never imagined them even knowing each other till they happened to come in together one day," the grey man observed. "She's all style and makeup, nice if you like that sort of thing, I suppose…"

The visitors didn't fail to notice the affectionate look that he gave the young assistant, who smiled in return despite having not apparently seen his expression.

"The fellow though, he's about as far from stylish as you could get," he continued.

"I don't know – is 'thug' a style?" mused the girl.

"Definitely sounds like the two we're after!" said Q with a grin.

"Vy for you want find them?" asked the girl.

Q and Wilko exchanged glances. There seemed no reason to be evasive.

There actually seemed to be something reassuring about the two in the shop. Whatever the relationship between them actually was, it radiated a quiet contentment as if both had found exactly what they were looking for in life.

"A mate of ours has gone missing, and we think they might have been the last people to see him. So anything you can tell us – names, addresses, anything that'd help us get in touch – would be really helpful," explained Wilko.

Now the two shop attendants did look at each other, and it was a look of concern.

"Ve cannot help much, I think. They not mention names, always pay cash so no plastic card details – Gregor is good at remembering details."

A smile creased the face under the lush greyness. Gregor clearly appreciated the compliment. But it faded in a moment and the look of concern returned.

"I wouldn't like to think the large fellow was last to see your friend. He is not a nice man."

Elizabeth looked concerned. "How do you know…?"

Gregor shrugged. "Sometimes you can just tell. Something in the movement, the voice, the attitude…"

"The vay he treats people. Vithout respect."

"He is like the old Russia," mused Gregor. "He has arrogance, based on strength rather than substance I think. Although…"

He went silent and looked blank, deep in thought.

Wilko and Q looked worried, but the girl made a calming gesture.

"He is thinking," she said, clearly used to his sudden moments of reverie.

Expression returned to Gregor's face, as if his mind had returned from a journey.

"A place called Mundara," he said. "There was one afternoon when the ugly fellow was here on his own. He already had a number of parcels and was buying quite a large amount from us. You were not here, Anna. You were – at the bank, I think. He had had a few vodkas I suspect, and was grumbling about having to carry so much. 'I should have this delivered,' he said. Then he looked at me and said, 'but you cannot deliver to Mundara. Nobody comes there!' and then he, well, laughed is not quite the word."

Q's pretty forehead creased as she said, "Mundara? Not a name I know. Wilko?"

The Tasmanian shrugged and shook his head.

"It is nowhere in Melbourne, I think. I have not heard of it," admitted the grey man.

"Nor I," added Anna.

"No other clues, then?" asked Q hopefully.

Anna spoke. "I remember vun thing he said. The big man, I mean. I vas talking to him vonce, as I put together his order. Making conversation, or trying to. I asked vat he vas doing in this country. He sounded – how to say – full of himself. 'Ve are doing important research on the mind,' he said. That stuck in my head as unlikely from him."

"He doesn't sound like the type for scientific research, I must admit," agreed Q.

Wilko thought about the ugly man he'd seen in *The Capital* and said, "A research subject, maybe. But he doesn't look the 'mind' type."

All four smiled – a relief of the tension that had quietly gripped all of them.

Wilko leaned to Anna and asked quietly, "Before we go – if you've got a nice spicy csabai amongst this lot, I'll take one, thanks?"

Anna smiled sweetly and said, "*Da*, sir – certainly."

Q handed over another of her business cards and said, "If you think of anything, please call me, okay?"

Gregor nodded, a slow and somber movement.

"We will. I hope you find your friend. I – wish you good luck," he said.

As she shook his hand, Elizabeth looked at him slightly askance. Just for a moment the grey-haired Russian had sounded like John B. Stewart. She felt a slight chill – the phrase 'someone walked over my grave' sprang to mind.

.o0o.

18 I FEAR THAT MAN HAS GONE AWAY

Later that night Q sat in her hotel room, scribbling ideas in a bound note-book she habitually carried.

Sometimes she'd look at what she'd just written, sigh, and draw a line through it. Other times she'd smile and draw a couple of stars beside it.

Unfortunately, she usually came back to those starred lines and crossed them out, too.

She looked up at the television and scowled. For reasons known only to the arcane gods of technology, on that particular night the only viewing options available were a True Crime cable channel, a Detective Mystery channel, a movie channel having a special *Death Wish/Dirty Harry* festi-val, and two news channels.

"Murder, mayhem and violence all round," she'd mused before settling on an English detective program in the hope of some humour.

A vain hope, as it had turned out. But in truth the television was really only on to try to muffle the sounds coming through the shared wall of the adjoining room.

It was like a recording of a thunderstorm that was being played through some high-tech sound equipment that distorted each rumble into a com-pletely different noise.

Elizabeth had never heard Wilko snore before. It was not something to be easily forgotten.

'Well, he's sleeping soundly – emphasis on the word *sound*,' she thought to herself. 'I'm glad *one* of us can.'

That thought led to further musing.

Why was this so important to her? John B. Stewart was nothing more than a friend to her. Wasn't he? Yes, his disappearance was a concern, but why take upon herself the role of chief investigator?

She knew why. She remembered a recent afternoon in the *Punters Folly*. "I wish you happiness, pretty lady," he'd said.

There was nothing grand in that sentence. Nothing romantic, no declaration of love. But she'd looked into his eyes as he spoke and what she saw was absolute sincerity.

It was disconcerting to realise that she couldn't remember anyone else ever saying that to her. Certainly not Sonny, who before they married, and for a while after, could be romantic in a clumsy, smitten-teenager sort of way. He always seemed to assume though that being with him would be happiness enough for her.

Obviously not her father Kevin – he'd left when she was very young and she really had no memories of him to call her own. All she knew was what her mother had told her, and that was filtered through a lot of bitterness and resentment.

Not even her mother, when she thought about it. "I just want you to be happy, dear," had been said often enough. It had almost been a mantra. But it had been a conditional happiness that was implied – "I want you to be happy *with me*" was the unspoken complete sentence.

It was as though Elizabeth had been expected to fill the void left in her mother's life when Kevin had taken off. Expected to fill it in perpetuity, it seemed.

Mother had died suddenly just a few months after the marriage to Sonny. "I just want you to be happy, dear," was what she'd said on the wedding day. But it was abundantly clear that she didn't like the young Mr. Dance.

But even though her assessment of his true character had proved to be correct, Elizabeth knew that the real reason for her mother's antipathy to her groom was jealousy. Someone else was to be the focus of her daughter's life.

"I wish you happiness." That was what John B. Stewart had said, and she knew that was what was meant. Too damn right she was going to find the man who'd said that to her. After she did – well, time would tell. At the very least they were already friends. Good friends, she realised. There's no such thing as too many good friends, and nobody can afford to give one up without an effort.

She tapped her pen on the notebook, enjoying that thought, and was startled when her mobile phone suddenly rang.

"Hello?" she said, after snatching the device up from her bedside table.

A crackly voice could be heard through a filter of static. "Elizabeth? Hi

– it's Darren here. Darren Bond? John's housemate…"

"I know who you are, Darren – it's alright…"

"Any news? Have you heard from John?"

"We haven't heard anything. I assume neither have you, since you're asking," she replied.

"Nothing. Listen, sorry about the late call, but I just got off work."

"It's okay mate, I understand your being concerned. I know how you feel." She paused and thought for a moment before saying, "Actually, if you're working the late shift and you've got some time up your sleeve during the day, there is something you might help with."

"Name it!" The young man's eagerness rang through the poor connection.

Elizabeth explained the conversations that she and Wilko had had that day in *The Capital* and the Balkan market.

"Could you try to find out where this 'Mundara' is? Wilko and I will be tied up in the office for most of the day. Check the computer, I'd reckon…"

There was a brief silence from the phone, before Darren's voice returned after a moment of thought.

"There's no computer here in the cottage. John never bothered to have one at home and I haven't got round to buying one. But there's the library. I could go over tomorrow and use one of the ones there. There are a few other resources I could check there too."

"You're okay to do that?" asked Elizabeth.

"Absolutely!" came the static-charged voice. "Scarlet taught me a bit about research while we were in Alice Springs. If it's the best thing I can do to help, then believe me, I'm on it!"

Q smiled and said, "Oh, I believe you, mate. Thank you! Give me a call when you can tomorrow, please."

As she put the phone back down a few moments later, Elizabeth smiled down at her notebook. She did believe Darren. She believed him because in his voice she heard genuine concern and loyalty. Emotion. Something that she strongly suspected could be heard in her own voice, too.

.o0o.

19 CROSSES TO BEAR

Earlier that evening the three expatriate Russians had stood in the kitchen of the Mundara house discussing what to try next on their 'guest'.

Solovyev was meticulously preparing the pastry cases for a batch of *perogi*. Aleksa was standing by the stove, stirring a pot of rice noodles. The doorway of the kitchen was substantially filled by Gleb's slouching form.

The burly Skripitsyn had been advocating that they dispose of Stewart. "Aleksa and I can take the boat to Melbourne tomorrow. Find a new subject – more than one. Aleksa and I are weary. Let us gather a new harvest. We can all benefit."

The doctor shook his head. "You suggest a handful of snacks when there is a feast to be had. Have patience, comrade," he replied.

The ugly man just stopped himself from spitting on the floor – he knew that he would be the one who would have to clean it up. "Pah! You keep saying this, but for three days now the procedure has not worked on him. Your 'feast' is in a locked room for which we do not have the key. Let us look for sustenance elsewhere!"

Solovyev paused in his work, contemplating his minion's complaint. "An interesting analogy," the doctor conceded. "I maintain, however, that this particular feast offers a far richer repast than any we have previously enjoyed. Perhaps, though, we might try another approach to the locked door. Aleksa? A woman's touch?"

Agony Aleksa shrugged. "If you think so," she said. "I wonder if Stewart has locked this door himself, or if there is somethink deeper here."

"You think his resistance may not be deliberate? An interesting notion," observed Dr. Solo.

"Unconscious, or rather subconscious, is what I was wonderink."

Solovyev turned and wiped his hands on a small towel.

"That is something you may be able to discern a clue to, my dear. I shall finish preparing these delicacies. Once you have done searching for chinks in Mr. Stewart's armour, as it were, please prepare him for another treatment. If you are successful, we may not need to increase the power any further this time. Then afterwards, the *perogi* can be fried and we can enjoy a good dinner, yes?"

"You know all that I want to consume," growled Gleb.

"Indeed, comrade," said Solo, patting his comrade's beefy arm. "I do understand, and your turn will come soon."

Aleksa laid aside the wooden spoon she had been using and left the kitchen. After first stopping at her own room to enhance her make-up she made her way to Stewart's room.

There she found John B. sitting cross-legged on his bed. He had opened his eyes as she'd entered the room.

"Is that the lotus position?" she asked with some amusement.

John B. looked up and shrugged. "It's a comfortable position," he replied. "I don't have a lot to distract myself with here, you might have noticed. A Hawaiian friend of mine taught me some meditation techniques."

"Ah – is that your secret, darlink?"

"Secret? No – it's just a way to pass the time. Keep calm and breathe."

"Mm. A simple enough form of mental discipline," she said, pondering that such a primitive process seemed unlikely to withstand Solovyev's technology.

"Don't knock simple. The simpler a thing is, the less there is to go wrong."

Aleksa sat on the bed beside the prisoner.

"You are a philosopher, darlink," she purred.

"That's not something I'm normally accused of," he said. "I'm just a simple bloke. I'll tell that to anyone who'll listen. But you and the walking toothpaste commercial don't seem to be listening."

"Toothpaste…? Ah – Doctor Solovyev." She laughed lightly and, it seemed, genuinely. "*Da*, he is a man who prides himself on his appearance."

"On your account?" asked John B.

Her smile froze momentarily. "No," she at last said with flat finality.

Stewart shrugged. The gesture could have meant anything. Aleksa regained her equilibrium.

"You are not so simple, Mr. Stewart. I think that your mind is quite – fas cinatink."

"Somebody once said that if the human brain was so simple that we could understand it, we'd be too simple to understand it."

Aleksa looked at him for a moment as she unraveled his sentence. Deciding to change tack slightly, she tried another line of seemingly innocuous questioning.

"How old are you, John darlink?"

John B. was just about to open his mouth to answer, when he glimpsed Aleksa's face reflected in the mirror on the dresser. He'd been carefully avoiding eye contact with the woman who was responsible for getting him into his current predicament. In the glass he saw a look best described as predatory. Whatever she was hungering for, he was disinclined to provide it.

So, as casually as he could he replied, "That's a rather personal question, isn't it?"

Aleksa's expression in the mirror betrayed a small knowing smile.

Stewart thought to himself, 'I wonder what it is that she and Solo know? Or that they think they do.'

Aleksa tried again. "What do you remember of your – early – life?"

There was something distinctly odd about the way she'd said that. Something more than could be attributed to her accent. He turned and, for the first time since she'd entered the room, looked her squarely in the eyes.

"Nothing special," he replied.

"Oh no. I think that you are most special," Aleksa answered, again slip-ping her voice into a purr.

As she did, she slid her hand along one of Stewart's crossed legs in a languid caress.

He didn't flinch or break their eye contact as he coldly said, "No. Don't kid yourself."

Her hand stopped its movement but wasn't removed from his leg. She looked surprised, if not hurt by his response.

"You do not find me – feminine?"

"Attractive, yes, I'll say that. But I do have some memory of how I got here, you know. And I have eyes and ears. I hear you and Solo talking, and the knuckle-dragger. With what you've been doing here, what you've admitted you've done without remorse, I'm not entirely sure I find you human."

Aleksa gave a little sigh and shrugged. She neither changed her position nor broke eye contact as with her other hand she jabbed the hypodermic needle into John B.'s leg.

He gave her a look as if to say, "See?" before his eyes glazed and his head dropped to his chest.

*

It wasn't a gradual awakening. It was sudden, and sharp. He was aware of a scratchy regular thudding noise. A regular $33^{1/3}$ beats per minute, if he'd counted them. He was awake, but not that lucid.

His first thought was, 'Wow – that vodka was potent! No, it was… whisky. Yes. Single malt. Ardbeg – meaning 'little bay' in Gaelic.'

It was the first time that he'd tried it, and he already knew it wouldn't be the last. He'd been quietly tippling cheap blended Scotch since soon after his fourteenth birthday, but now, almost two years later, this was like an epiphany.

'Gotta thank Ferret's brother for getting it for me – what a great birthday present,' he thought.

With that thought he opened his eyes to look for his mate Ferret. He was easy to find – both teenagers had fallen asleep ('passed out' would be a harsher, if more accurate, term) in their chairs.

The large armchairs furnished the lounge of the "granny flat" on the downstairs level of Ferret's family home. The flat had accommodated first Grandmamma, then Ferret's older brother Paul. Since Paul had flown the parental nest it had been turned over to the younger sibling Vivian, who hated his given name and was much happier being known by the nickname his size and thin features had inspired.

Both brothers were growing up with minimal intervention (or discipline or even guidance) from their determinedly Modern parents. If Ferret wanted to have friends over to visit, that was fine. If they stayed up all night reading comics and playing records that was fine, too. The flat was well insulated so the sound wouldn't carry upstairs.

John B. peered at the scrawny figure curled up in the chair opposite him. Yes, Ferret was breathing. That was alright then.

Next he identified the source of the rhythmic sound. The 'Auto Stop' function of the turntable clearly wasn't working and the stylus was wearing itself away on the inner circle of the Beatles album still revolving on the record player. The last song he remembered hearing was *Hey Jude*.

Stewart got up from his chair, a little unsteadily, and turned off the machine. Ferret still didn't stir.

John B. yawned and stretched expansively. He picked up a handful of *Conan the Barbarian* comics from the floor and settled back into the armchair.

"I wouldn't mind living like this," he said quietly to himself.

His parents – well, the couple he called his parents – were older than Ferret's mother and father, both in years and attitude. Staying out overnight, even on a Friday with no school the next day, was out at the very furthest extent of permitted behavior.

They only wanted the best for him. At heart, he knew that. But his adolescent perception of what was 'best' rather differed from theirs. The relaxed 'anything goes' lifestyle that Paul and Ferret enjoyed looked more than appealing.

He wasn't to know that within eighteen months both brothers would die of drug overdoses, a sad fact about which his adoptive father at least had the grace not to say, "I told you so."

That was still in the unguessed future. On this early Saturday morning, idly perusing the adventures of the brawny hero and sundry scantily-clad buxom wenches, John B. just thought it would be nice to not feel pressured all the time. Study hard, make something of yourself, live up to your potential – that was the mantra.

It was why he'd taken to drink. Two years ago he'd been taken to a 21st birthday party, for the son of an old family friend. He'd been allowed to try a couple of alcoholic drinks on the assumption that the taste of neat spirits would be too strong for him and would put him off drinking for a while.

Fourteen-year-old John B. was shrewd enough to play along with that, but had actually realised that Scotch in particular was good at taking the edge off the stress he felt under. What's more, it tasted pretty damn fine.

Study hard, make something of yourself, live up to your potential – 'don't fail' was what he heard. Exams and tests had come easily to him early in his schooling, but the more pressure he felt himself under, the more difficult they'd become.

Sheer bravado had taken him into a bottle shop run by a man with a reputation around the school for turning a blind eye to the age of his customers. A half bottle of decent blended Scotch turned out to be just the thing for getting through end-of-year exams.

Of course now he'd just discovered single malt whisky. The bar had been raised, so to speak – thanks, Paul! The money from the Saturday morning supermarket job due to start in a couple of weeks was already being earmarked. Goodness knows, his regular small allowance wouldn't stretch to this luxury.

Ferret shifted in his chair. John B. could hear his gentle snoring.

Study hard, make something of yourself, live up to your potential – no such pressure on lucky Ferret! What was that line he'd read in a *Peanuts* cartoon?

Ah yes. "There's no heavier burden than a great potential," he said to himself.

"*Mais non, monsieur!* The great potential that this account offers you is no burden at all! I promise, it will be very much to your advantage."

He looked across the desk at the banker, who was almost as immaculately turned out as he was himself.

"Indeed. Pardon, Monsieur Bernardin – it was a momentary distraction. Your service does seem to meet my requirements."

"*Certainement.* We offer security, good returns, and of course, our absolute discretion. You have a substantial amount that you wish to deposit?"

The blonde Russian nodded and smiled a perfect smile at the urbane Frenchman as he replied, "Yes, a satisfactory sum."

That was an understatement. There had been more of the Dashkov family estate left by his brothers Mikhail and Vladimir than he'd expected, and the liquidation of the assets had reaped a substantial return.

But that had been only the beginning.

Vladimir Rastorguyev had noted Tretyakov's continuing vigour as his own faded, particularly after the war. The merchant had guessed correctly that his business partner was somehow applying to himself some version of the treatment that had made their agriculture concerns so successful.

The senior partner had pleaded to be included in the secret. The scientist eventually agreed, on condition that he be named sole heir to the business. The ailing merchant readily agreed – he had neither wife nor offspring, and his brothers were already dead.

Rastorguyev responded well to the stimulatory procedure without understanding the nature of what was being done. That ignorance was his undoing. A year or so after writing the will that favoured Tretyakov he was quite oblivious to the subtle changes that his new heir made to his 'treatment'.

It was left to the business' new sole owner to regretfully explain to the assembled employees that his esteemed partner had succumbed to one of the dreadful debilitating illnesses that so often accompanied the Russian winter. How terrible it was that it had happened so quickly.

Konstantin had taken his cue from Lenin's return to Petrograd in disguise and his subsequent rise to power. He again saw the balance of power shifting, as it had done from the aristocrats to the merchants. Now it was clear that the merchant class were becoming perceived as the enemies of the state.

He quietly sold off the elements of the business. The herds, the pastures and the processing factories all fetched good prices. The Rastorguyev brand had developed a fine reputation over the decades. What he didn't sell was the secret behind much of that reputation and the equipment that facilitated it. He would put no price on his own genius.

It had been time for Konstantin Solovyev to emerge in the place of Konstantin Tretyakov. It was a time of chaos, when old identities could be readily lost and replaced with new ones.

It was a time when a shrewd man might identify someone in the emerging political machine who was intelligent enough to see the potential of covert research. Revolutionary jargon might speak of 'power to the people' but the reality was that power was, as ever, to be in the hands of certain select people. And a key to that was finding new and better ways of manipulating and subjugating those other people.

Solovyev was making a place for himself alongside, if not actually within, the new All-Russian Extraordinary Commission for Struggle Against Counter-Revolution and Sabotage. The *Cheka*, which was in effect a secret police force. Already, it was recognizably a force that would make full use of mercenaries and other 'contractors'.

He knew that his monetary reward for providing new and efficient ways of extracting information from subjects would not be great. However state sanction of his research – his true research that 'information extraction' was a mere cover for – would be invaluable.

Financial reward was not important to him anyway. He was not short of money, although that in itself was a potential problem that would have to be addressed. Conspicuous wealth was a dangerous liability in the new Russia. Even, or perhaps especially for a man who was inveigling his way deep into the shadowy affairs that lay under the Cheka.

There were private banks in France that catered for the small but significant clientele across Europe who wanted their money well secured from the prying eyes and grasping hands of government.

The Tretyakov fortune was about to find a new home where it would be secure from whatever vagaries may lie in the future of Mother Russia. "You may of course discreetly draw upon it at any time, but your satisfactory sum will be safe with us for as long as you wish it so, Monsieur Solovyev. *Aussi longtemps que c'est necessaire*," said Bernardin.

The perfect smile continued to dazzle the banker.

"As long as is necessary, yes, thank you Monsieur Bernardin. I anticipate that this will be a long term investment. Very long term, in fact. And please, monsieur, I am *Doctor* Solovyev."

The professional title was a sudden whim. Despite his impressive education Konstantin had no such formal qualification. He'd never needed it. He knew now that he never would. But it suited his self-image, he realised, just as he realised that his self-image was the most important thing in the world.

In the basement of the Mundara house Aleksa looked up from her control panel. The dials had flickered into ranges even she had never seen before.

Surely this time it had worked?

  She looked across the room. The contented smile on Dr. Solo's face

seemed to bear out her optimism. But as she left her desk to remove the

skullcap from the blonde head she stopped short.

  The unconscious John B. Stewart wore the same contented smile.

.o0o.

20 NOT MUCH HELP DESK

Before going into the office for the morning focus meeting Wilko and Elizabeth had presented themselves at a police station near the hotel.

There they were 'assisted' by Constable Iglesias, the day's duty desk officer.

"So what's the address of this missing person?" he asked in a voice devoid of interest.

Wilko provided the details of John B.'s Waramanga cottage.

"Waramanga? That's not local," observed the policeman.

"No, it's in Canberra. We *said*, he was here working but hasn't come home…" Elizabeth began.

"So he's missing from Canberra, not Melbourne. You'll have to talk to the police there. Not our problem, sorry," he said in a voice that made it clear he was not in the least sorry.

"But he went missing from here, in town…"

The dark haired policeman's tone shifted from disinterest to thinly veiled hostility. "We have no way of knowing that. He hasn't turned up at home, so that's where he's missing from. When, or if, the Canberra police get in touch I'm sure we'll do our best to help with their enquiries."

They weren't to know that Constable Bruno Iglesias was himself an ex-Canberran who'd had several applications to join the Federal Police there turned down. He would rather have shot all the toes off his own right foot than help anyone from the nation's capital.

Elizabeth took a deep breath, counted to ten and said, "Alright. We can make our own enquiries. For a start, can you point us in the direction of a place called Mundara?"

"Nope. Never heard of it."

"Do you think you might try looking it up?" The steel in Elizabeth's voice made even the recalcitrant Iglesias squirm uncomfortably in his seat.

He reached for a directory under his counter. "You got a postcode?" he asked.

Wilko shook his head. "No. It's…"

"Too small I suppose," interrupted the surly constable. "M U double N dara was it?"

"One N," corrected the pretty brunette. "It's…"

"Can't see it in the jurisdiction list. No idea which station is responsible for it. Not in Melbourne anyway. Suppose it could be one of the country stations. Oh, wait. Here's the name. It's an island. Out in Bass Strait."

"Thank you," Elizabeth finally managed to say with teeth-clenched politeness.

The constable looked up from the book that he closed with a snap.

"Ah well then – there's your problem, especially if that's where your missing mate has gone. Probably over the state border – it'll be a Tasmanian matter. You want to watch out – they're a weird mob down there."

Q grabbed Wilko's arm and squeezed, wordlessly stopping him from replying or doing more than a momentary goldfish impression.

"We'll be on our way then," she said to the policeman. "I'd like to thank you for all your help."

"What help?" asked Iglesias, confused.

She gave him a humourless smile and replied, "That's right," before leading Wilko out of the station.

As they headed for the office he turned to her and said, "Well, that was a whole lot less use than I'd hoped."

She grimaced. "If I had that magic power of John B.'s I'd have wished for something appropriate for that guy."

"Hmph. Bloody 'magic'. But I agree with the sentiment."

A little corner of Wilko's mind noted that Elizabeth had used John's middle initial – something that normally only Stewart himself did. He was pretty sure she hadn't even noticed. But she did keep saying they were 'just good friends' and sounded sincere about it.

He settled for continuing, "Have you any thoughts on what we do next?"

"We wait, I guess. Keep asking questions when we can, and keep our eyes and ears open. Maybe Darren will come up with something."

.o0o.

21 BOOKWORK

Darren scratched his head, completely unaware that the gesture made him look like a young Stan Laurel.

He tapped the now-worn point of his pencil on the open notebook beside him. He was sitting at a carrel in the Undergraduate Library of the Australian National University.

Earlier in the day he'd put in an hour or two of work in the National Library trying to find information about Mundara.

It wasn't quite as elusive as Cobbemarmoo had seemed to be when he'd been conducting similar research in the Alice Springs library in the Northern Territory. There was at least some basic information.

It was a small island – less than half a square mile in area. It was a lump of granite sitting out in Bass Strait, just a little south of the invisible line in the water that was the 'official' border between Victoria and Tasmania.

At least four species of skinks made their home on the island, along with some blue-tongued lizards, according to naturalists who had visited Mundara in the past. They lived among lush vegetation that thrived on a small natural spring and plenty of rainwater.

Darren had chuckled when he read how the weather had given the island its name. An early European captain had been sailing between the main land and Tasmania. On board he had a couple of natives who he hoped would be helpful with navigation. As a not uncommon Bass Strait storm had raged around them the captain had seen the blurry shape of the island through the rain.

"What is that?" he'd asked, expecting that one of the locals might recognize the place.

Unhappy at being on the open water during a big storm, the native hadn't even looked in the direction the captain was pointing. Huddled miserably under a soaking canvas he'd replied, "Mundara."

And so the captain had recorded what he thought was the island's name, unaware that his navigator had instead been using his own language's word for the 'thunder' that had been rolling overhead.

All of which was at least a bit interesting, but didn't offer much towards finding the missing wizard.

What really puzzled Darren was that every reference he'd found to Mundara indicated that the island was uninhabited. But Elizabeth had given the definite impression that someone lived there – someone who knew something about what had happened to his best friend.

He'd allowed himself a short break in the library coffee shop. He'd sat with a cappuccino and a newspaper he barely glanced at, instead looking pensively out through the glass wall.

The young, very blonde waiter had seen the worried look on his customer's face and in a quiet moment asked if there was a problem he could help with. The gesture of kindness touched Darren – he hadn't realised how alone he felt in John B.'s unexplained absence. Alone and vulnerable.

The waiter's concern turned out to be genuine, not just the politeness of a well-trained hospitality worker. He listened to Darren's explanation of what he'd been looking for (and a very edited version of why).

"You ought to try the library at the ANU. There's a lot of the same stuff as here, but you can also look at some government stuff that's supposed to be restricted access, if you know how," offered the waiter.

Darren's smile was a thin one. "That'd be great, if I did know how."

His new confidante looked around a little furtively then asked, "Have you a pen and paper handy?" When the requested items were put on the table he wrote a couple of web addresses and, beside them, some odd combinations of characters. "Passwords into a couple of useful sites," he explained.

Darren frowned, first at the paper then at his benefactor. "How do you know…?" he began.

The young blonde man shrugged. "I'm studying political science at ANU. We… learn stuff. Sometimes officially, sometimes not." He held out a hand. "I'm Malcolm. They call me Goldie. As in Goldilocks. It's the hair…"

Darren's puzzled frown was replaced by a broad grin. "I get it. I'm Darren. They call me Darren." He shook the proffered hand. "Thanks for your help, Goldie – I was thinking I'd hit a dead end."

The grin got a warm smile in return. "You're welcome. Listen, if you need any more help finding your friend, just call me and I'll see if I can think of anything." The blonde grabbed the pen and added a mobile phone number to the paper on the table.

Darren was about to protest that he didn't have a mobile himself, but stopped. 'I wanted to get one anyway,' he thought. 'I can use a public phone in the meantime if I have to.'

He pocketed the piece of paper. "Thanks mate – I really appreciate it," he said.

Goldie's smile had widened. "You're welcome, Darren. Keep in touch, hey? I hope those sites help."

They had. After the bus trip across town he'd settled into the University library, and Goldie's tips had opened up just a little bit of information that he'd diligently transferred into his notebook.

Now he sat in the carrel, looking at his notes and trying to extract something he thought might be truly useful. He couldn't see it.

He didn't know much about Elizabeth Dance. They'd met once in the *Punters' Folly*. Spoken a couple of times on the phone. When John had mentioned her it was as a friend, although now that he thought of it there was a certain fondness in his housemate's voice when he did.

But she'd impressed the young man. Her concern for his best friend was obvious and genuine. She was clearly determined and well-organised. He tapped the pencil again.

"Well," he said to himself – very quietly, being respectful of sitting in a library – "I've done what I can. I just hope Wilko and Elizabeth can do something with it. And that John's okay. If he's somehow got stuck out on this Mundara place, well that's pretty weird, and I've seen weird around John before. It's not good."

.o0o.

22 CROSS BREEDING

Aleksa turned slightly from where she stood at the sink washing the breakfast dishes and looked at the doctor sitting listlessly on a kitchen stool.

"You did not sleep well," she observed.

Solovyev nodded and took a deep breath.

"A bad dream?" she enquired politely.

"Not this time."

Aleksa didn't visibly react but made a small mental note of his answer.

Doctor Solo continued, his voice a little slower than usual as he assembled his thoughts.

"I have recollections of comic books and… unfamiliar music. I believe
I am getting *something* from Mister Stewart, but the experience is unlike
any we have encountered before."

"Is he really so unique an individual?"

"I think he is that rarest of creatures, Aleksa – a genetic prototype."

Yusupova placed a cup on the drainer and turned to face the doctor properly, her expression somewhere between intrigue and skepticism.

She said, "He hardly looks like it."

Solovyev didn't meet her gaze, but neither did he seem to be deliberately
avoiding it. He was staring into an unknown distance, clearly turning

things over in his mind – analyzing and theorizing.

Eventually he replied, "It is misguided, even dangerous, to ascribe too much to physical features. However much you and I appreciate the aesthetics of appearance, only a fool, like that conceited corporal who ran Germany into disaster, believes that looks in any way denote perfection. The true purity is in the mind. True purity and true power. That is the foundation of my work. Our work. Look at Gleb."

"Must I?" Aleksa said with a trace of a smile.

"Ah, familiarity does breed contempt. You know as well as I do that behind that unattractive exterior there is a powerful brain. If his surprising early test results were not proof enough, his subsequent capacity to assimilate benefit from the procedure surely is."

"As you say." The doctor's confidante sounded unimpressed as she turned back to her chore and said, "I might wish that such a mind were put to better use."

"You suggest perhaps that Gleb might himself be a suitable subject for the – other end of the procedure? Potentially, yes, that would be the case. But he is useful in many ways, and, dear Aleksa, I do value loyalty. I have found that loyalty is most effective when it is mutual."

If Yusupova detected a barb in the remark she gave no evidence of it, instead replying, "Useful, yes. His brawn is useful, and he does have an affinity for machines that is of benefit both in the laboratory and elsewhere. I concede his value in maintainink equipment."

"Such as our very important boat that he is currently cleaning the motor of. Comrade Skripitsyn has a fondness for that particular piece of equipment. I think that to him it is a link to a world that he misses – a world beyond Mundara."

That struck a resonant chord with Aleksa. It was one she chose not to acknowledge openly to the doctor.

"You mentioned receivink somethink from Stewart. Is it these dreams you are havink?"

Solovyev nodded slowly. "They may be a manifestation. Brief fragments that fade quickly. I believe that I am deriving some energy from our subject, but I wonder if during the transference I am acquiring something more?"

"I must tell you, Doctor, from my observations durink the procedure the process does not appear to be – strictly one way."

"That seems unusual. I would go so far as to call it unlikely. The equipment was not designed to operate in such a manner, as you well know."

"Indeed. However I can only report to you what I am witnessink. The instruments do show that energy is flowink from him to you, but the readings fluctuate quite wildly, no matter what settinks I have tried. The gauges are not designed to register transference in the opposite direction. It was not a possibility which we had discussed."

"Not one we had considered, Aleksa, I must confess. Then again, happening upon an individual like Mr. Stewart could hardly have been predicted."

Dr. Solo inhaled deeply and pulled himself upright, gathering up his energy and determination.

"We will not wait for Gleb to return. Aleksa, please go downstairs and prepare the machines. I will see to our guest myself. I feel we should push on and push through as local parlance puts it. Perhaps rather than merely increasing the current overall, we should try a different configuration to target particular parts of his brain for greater or lesser intensity of the procedure."

With a carefully neutral, "As you wish, Comrade Doctor," Aleksa pulled the plug from the sink, meticulously dried her hands and walked from the kitchen without a backward glance.

Solovyev watched her pass and as she left the room said under his breath, "I think that you are challenging me too, in your own way, dear Aleksa. I may need Mr. Stewart's strength, *nyet*?"

*

Rhythm. Rhythm. Always there was the rhythm.

It was the sound of marching feet. Hundreds of them. The Red Army paraded around the square for the approval of their leader who was watching from the balcony.

Having just been ushered into the most secure office in the country then left alone by an aide-de-camp, the blonde doctor sat and waited patiently in a comfortable chair. Soon enough, the commander-in-chief returned from reviewing the troops and sat behind his vast desk.

"The war goes well," he announced, stroking his moustache over a smile.

Even for the sanguine Solovyev this seemed a remarkable statement, given the enormous loss of life Russia had sustained. But he was careful not to let emotion or surprise show as the President continued.

"Beria sends me good reports of your work, Comrade Doctor. The functions of the Peoples Commissariat for Internal Affairs are apparently enhanced by the results of your research."

"Thank you, Comrade. The NKVD has given me the encouragement and support I require – I am happy to render service in return. Comrade? Is something wrong?"

The President was staring, puzzled, at his guest.

"My – apologies, Doctor. You are significantly younger than I expected. I had understood from Comrade Beria that the Solovyev Institute had been, as you put it 'rendering service' for twenty years."

The blonde man smiled his perfect smile. "I am Konstantin Konstantinovich Solovyev. I took up my father's work upon his passing," he lied smoothly. He had been expecting such a question eventually.

"Indeed? I have seen no record of his death." Clearly the President had examined such files as he had before meeting the shadowy NKVD 'scientific advisor' for the first time.

"Our family does not court publicity. We have always been humble ser vants of the State, applying ourselves to the best of our ability. My father trained me well, so for our work the transition was a seamless one. As to the official records I cannot say. The years before the War had their – complications, did they not?”

The great leader sat back in his chair, looking contemplative. The early years of the NKVD had indeed been difficult although this was not publicized. It was only when Beria took charge in 1938 that things became well organized. He gave an internal mental shrug. What other reasonable explanation could there be? Clearly the man in front of him was not fifty years old or more. What did it matter, so long as the appropriate results were being achieved?

He stroked his moustache again, an unconscious habit whenever he reached a decision.

“So. I am pleased to meet at least one of the Doctors Solovyev at last. Beria reports that your techniques for information extraction yield excellent results.”

“Thank you, Comrade. I should acknowledge the valuable input of the new assistant furnished to me by the NKVD in this regard.”

The President closed his eyes in a moment of concentration. “Yusupova? Yes. Academically gifted young woman. She comes from one of the old elite families who – fell with the demise of the Tsar. In your opinion is she to be trusted?”

Solovyev smiled. “I am impressed by her loyalty, Comrade. And as you say, she has a fine intellect. She seems to enjoy her work."

There was a slow satisfied nod from across the broad desk.

"Excellent. As to that work, there is a reason I wished to meet with you privately. There is some – indication in what I have read that some of your research may be applied to improving the resilience of our personnel."

"Resistance to disease? Yes, possibly," admitted the doctor, carefully avoiding any suggestion of resistance to aging. He knew this was not a secret to be shared with so ruthless a leader.

"Pursue this line of research, Doctor Solovyev," came the order.

"To the exclusion of other research?"

"For now, yes. The Commissariat's interrogative processes are now working adequately."

"Disease was certainly the most prolific killer of the Great War," said Solovyev.

"Uncontrolled, random disease," observed the President. "I believe that we will soon see new ways of conducting warfare. Biological weapons. We already have teams researching such possibilities for our own use. Such work would be futile however were I not to also address the matter of immunity to such weapons. An all-purpose immunity."

Solovyev noted the subtle, perhaps unconscious change in his leader's use of pronouns.

"I understand," he said.

The President nodded. "Understand too that our Allies are squeamish about the idea. I think the British regard it as ungentlemanly. I wish your research to remain a well kept secret."

"I am used to working covertly. Comrade Beria…"

"Even Beria is to know nothing of this!"

The doctor's handsome features betrayed a trace of surprise at his commander's sudden vehemence.

"There are those even within my senior ranks who do not share my views on the potential, or inevitability of such warfare. In this matter, your work is to be conducted for me, and me alone. The head of the NKVD will be made aware that you have a new line of authority. It will be a direct line, but a most discreet one. Do you understand?"

"Completely, Comrade."

It was clear that for all his current favoured position, Beria was not completely trusted. 'Not unwise – he's a cunning and ruthless man,' mused Solovyev. 'And such similar personalities would do well to be wary of one another.'

Aloud the doctor continued, "I may require additional resources to enable my change of priority. Especially if my work is to be conducted away from Commissariat scrutiny."

"It shall be arranged."

Solovyev's inner smile was even brighter than the one he turned on his chief. This was no 'change of priority' at all – not of his own true priority, at least. He looked forward to concentrating more fully on harnessing the great power he already knew bio-electricity could offer. The nature of the communication he would allow to flow to his commander would have to be carefully managed, of course. But he was confident in his own ability and experience.

"I am profoundly grateful for the opportunity," he said.

'What a strange manner of speech for a schoolboy,' thought the Curator, looking down at the purple-shirted lad standing in his cluttered office.

Rather awkwardly he replied, "Well, er, yes. Good. It's not every child who gets a behind-the-scenes tour of the Museum."

The boy was smiling brightly at him.

'Ah yes,' the Curator remembered. The school had mentioned he seemed an intelligent child. Apparently he'd read voraciously during his time in the orphanage, and his new parents encouraged his frequent visits to the library. 'It explains how he won the Museum's essay competition, I suppose.'

"Thank you, Mr. Johnson. Where will we start?"

Wallace Johnson returned the smile. The boy's voice seemed more normal now.

"Where would you like, young John? Do you have a particular field of interest?"

"Hmm – history, I think."

"Good-o. Australian history?"

"The world, sir!" young Stewart replied enthusiastically.

"Well, that's rather a broad canvas I'm afraid. Let's narrow it down a little, shall we?"

The boy looked thoughtful.

"I'd like to see things that are really, really old. Not fossils and stuff, but things people actually made and used," he finally said.

Johnson laughed out loud. "Good man! You've come to the right place!"

Wallace's pleasure was genuine. Childless himself, he appreciated an enquiring young mind eager to share in the things that he had been interested in all his life.

Thumbs tucked in the lapels of his brown tweed coat, he led the way through the maze of corridors and rooms that made up much of the less visible elements of the Museum. He pushed open a door and entered one of his favourite rooms.

Waving an expansive arm to show off the room's contents he said, "This is where we keep the elements of ancient Greek civilization which aren't presently on public display. We have…"

Curator Johnson stopped, suddenly realizing he was talking to himself. He looked around and realised that the boy had gone into a small anteroom just inside the entrance. Wallace smiled as he noted that the small hands weren't actually touching anything, indeed they were scrupulously clasped behind the lad's back.

Perhaps unconsciously he duplicated the young student's pose as he stepped into the small room.

Smiling, he said, "Ah, what you've found here is our Carthaginian collection. Rather smaller than what we have of the Greeks I'm afraid. An interesting people, nonetheless. Carthage was a colony of the people we call Phoenician. They invented a twenty-two character alphabet that the Greeks later adopted – or rather, adapted themselves."

"I've heard of them, sir. The Phoenicians were sailors, weren't they?"

"Very good, lad, so they were. Not one race, as such – there was no country called Phoenicia. The term referred to people from a region around what is now Lebanon, from a number of city states such as Tyre and Sidon."

The boy nodded. "Those are names I know from the Bible. For a while I didn't have much else to read in the Home. There was a… connection with the Canaanites?"

"Ye-e-es," said Wallace slowly. "I confess that I don't recall that link being referred to in the Scriptures but yes, the Canaanites are considered by some historians to be the ancestors of the Phoenicians. Not something I would expect a young man of your age to be aware of, frankly."

"Sorry sir, it just sort of, well, popped into my head."

"No apology necessary, my young friend." The Curator looked very thoughtful. His next words could have been in reference to the boy's potential or his past – in truth he couldn't have said which, if not both. "You could be anything."

Young John B. smiled. "I think that all I want to be is content," he re plied.

There was something wistful about Wallace Johnson's face as he said gravely, "I wish you the best of luck with that, lad. You may find that a more difficult ambition than it should be."

There was something of that implied longing reflected in Solovyev's features as Aleksa disconnected the apparatus from his scalp.

"A different reaction at least," she mused aloud. "But I think not yet the one that we are lookink for."

"A… difficult ambition…" said the doctor softly.

.oOo.

23 THERE ARE FACTS, AND THERE ARE IDEAS

The sun had set in Melbourne on what had been another distracted day of consultation with department staff, some of whom had wondered aloud, "Whatever happened to John B. Stewart?"

The two facilitators, after one quick round of drinks at the *Capital*, had returned to their hotel. Darren had rung to report what he'd discovered just as they'd stepped out of the elevator and the Tasmanian quickly opened up his room for them.

Now Elizabeth and Wilko stared thoughtfully at the mobile phone on the room's miniscule desk.

"Hello? Are you still there?" came the young man's voice, crackling through the loudspeaker setting of the little device.

'Loudspeaker' was a misleading title, as the louder the volume was set to, the less like speech were the sounds that came out.

"Sorry mate, we're thinking," answered Elizabeth.

"That's okay. I was just worried I'd lost you somehow. I only bought the phone today and I'm still getting used to it."

"Well, you're ahead of John, at least," observed Wilko. "If he had a bloody mobile we could have rung him days ago and just asked him where the hell he is."

"Assuming he could answer it," Darren replied. "I mean, I reckon that if he could get to a phone at all he'd have called by now."

Elizabeth looked unhappy. "I think you're right," she said. "The more time passes the more I can't help thinking the worst. Those two creepy Russians are the closest we've got to any lead at all, and they're leading us to an uninhabited island."

"I guess so," said the tinny voice emanating from Canberra. "I mean, I guess it's uninhabited. It was when it was some kind of national park. There's a record of a Ranger's house but nobody was posted to live in it for quite a while. And then, like I said, the place just sort of fell off the department records a few years ago."

"No record of sale?" asked Elizabeth, confirming a note she'd scribbled down earlier in Darren's call.

"Nothing I could find. One year there's a single line entry in a register, next year not even that. I wonder if – hey! What are you doing?"

Darren's voice was directed away from the phone, obviously in reaction to a series of peculiar thumps that were loud enough to be audible through Elizabeth's phone.

"Hang on, please," the young man said. "I'd better see what's up with Kat. Sounds like he's fallen in the bath."

"Quick! Don't let him drown!" cried Elizabeth.

Wilko looked worried too. "Yeah – John'd be really p..."

"It's alright, there's no water in..." Darren's voice trailed off for a mo ment. "What are you doing, you crazy animal?"

"What's going on?" asked Wilko, who was more fond of the big white Persian than he often let on.

"He's chasing the boat around the empty tub."

"You have a boat in the bathtub? How big is it?" asked Elizabeth.

"The boat or the tub?" returned the distracted Darren.

"Either."

"Give it here, Kat – thank you – sorry Elizabeth. It's a normal sized bath, and a little floating soap holder in the shape of a yacht. Souvenir of Tasmania it says on the side."

"That thing? John's still got it?" Wilko sounded surprised. "I brought that back for him from a trip home years ago. One of the times I was down there watching the end of the Sydney to Hobart yacht race. I thought that would have been long lost by now."

"Oh no, he's more careful than that. John's a bit sentimental about presents from friends, you know," came the voice from the Canberra cottage.

  Wilko reddened slightly. Admitting his own or anyone else's sentiment didn't come easily to him.

"So – sorry about the interruption. Where were we at?" Darren continued.

"A dead end," Wilko answered flatly.

"Maybe not," said Elizabeth with a glint in her eye that made Wilko suddenly nervous.

  She fixed a thoughtful stare on the Tasmanian. "You go down to watch the race – have you ever sailed?”

“No! Well, yes, I’ve sailed – quite a bit, actually – but never in the big race. I would have liked to, I suppose,” he replied, his voice perhaps betraying a little regret.

“But you *can* sail?”

“Yes.”

“Good. I can drive a boat – Sonny was keen on water-skiing for a while.”

“You water-skied?” asked Darren, a little intrigued by the image, as his only experience of the sport was watching the scantily clad trick performers at a water park show.

“Not after the first couple of attempts,” the brunette admitted. “I really didn’t enjoy the impact of the water when I came down. I decided that I should drive the boat and let Sonny have all the salt water enemas he wanted.”

  Both Wilko and Darren winced at the mental picture.

“Anyway, the point is,” she continued, “I can handle a boat, and you can handle a boat. Darren’s given us the location of where this Mundara is. We hire a boat, go over there, and find John. Sounds like the island’s not that big.”

“About three kilometres by less than two at the longest and widest bits,” confirmed the voice from Canberra.

  Wilko was doing the impression of a goldfish that happened when he was thoroughly disconcerted. “Wait on, wait on!” he said. “We’re supposed to be flying back to Canberra tomorrow afternoon, aren't we? Job done, report back to Kaiser Ron?"

"I can get flights changed easily enough. I booked them, remember. And I'll deal with Ron, too. We've done the job we promised him. But let's face it, the three of us know that's not really the job we came for."

"The island's fifty miles out into Bass Strait. That's a really nasty stretch of water!" Wilko continued to protest, although he already knew he was wasting his breath.

Elizabeth raised her eyebrows at him. "The ugly Russian guy can manage the trip single-handed, from what we've heard. I don't see why you and I can't manage it between us."

"I can think of a whole list of reasons, but that's not going to stop you, is it?" sighed Wilko, resignedly.

Down the phone, Darren sounded uncertain. "Um… I can only wish you luck. I reckon that'd be more effective coming from John though."

Elizabeth gave a little smile at the memory of a wished-for dragon. "Maybe," she said. "But you've done your bit, mate. We find John, and you know it'll be thanks to you."

In a cottage in Canberra the young man looked at his new mobile phone with considerable concern and thought to himself, 'If the two of you disappear out in Bass Strait somewhere that'll be thanks to me, too, won't it?'

.oOo.

24 CROSSING LINES

John B. pushed the soup bowl away, its contents untouched.

"I'm sure that it's bloody good borscht, as borscht goes, but I'm not a fan of beetroot even when I have a decent appetite for dinner," he said.

Dr. Solovyev smiled politely.

"No offence taken," he said. "I had thought, however, that Australians were among the few in the world to embrace the humble beetroot nearly as enthusiastically as we Eastern Europeans."

"I've been told it's good in salads and on hamburgers. Not for me though – it tastes like a mouthful of damp dirt," replied the wizard.

"Eating dirt is all you are worthy of," growled Gleb before swallowing a spoonful of soup.

With a safe distance of table between them Stewart mildly replied, "Based on the idea that we are what we eat, I'd have thought that was more your diet, Grub."

The ugly enforcer's face turned the colour of his soup.

Aleksa put a restraining hand on the big man's arm. "He is challengink you, Gleb. Do not rise to his bait."

"Challenge – pah! I could tear him to pieces. And so I should…"

"*Not* before I am done with him!" said Solo emphatically. "He challenges

because it his nature. He antagonizes you hoping to exploit a weakness.
That is clearly his strategy. Do you wonder if the machines are up to the
challenge that you are proving to be, Mr. Stewart?"

Gleb turned his glower on the doctor and said, "I think the 'challenge'
means more to you than the result. You are deriving enough to sustain
you, *da*? But we – Aleksa and I - are forgotten. We *need* to be revived!"
"And so you shall be. We have here a singular resource, not an insur-
mountable problem. You believe you are capable of meeting any physical
challenge from our guest, and while I suspect he may surprise you…"
he raised a conciliatory hand at his comrade, "I also believe you would
prevail. I likewise believe that the procedure will prevail. Yes, the results
thus far have been – anomalous. But that only reinforces my conviction
that the prize will be worth the pursuit. Our equipment, not to mention our
persistence, is being challenged but the machines will overcome."
Aleksa's voice sounded weary. "Redesignink and reconfigurink them
to record, let us call it *reverse* transference, would be an onerous and
time-consumink task that I admit, I do not feel I have the energy for."
The doctor nodded, genuine in his sympathy. Despite the reserve of his
manner, Yusupova and Skripitsyn were the closest things he had to friends.
Primarily they were useful, yes, but long familiarity had also brought a
degree of fondness - as much as Konstantin could feel such emotion for
anyone beyond himself.
"Recording the data would perhaps be a waste of resources," he conceded.

"How many other subjects like him are we likely to encounter? He is the first, indeed the only one in almost a century of work to prove so difficult."

"Pardon me for not making your life easier. It's not deliberate I do assure you," said John B. with labored mock politeness. Then his forehead creased as Solovyev's words sunk in. "Hang on. A century of work? Are you carrying on a proud family tradition or something?"

"A proud tradition, yes, but not quite 'family' tradition. I see you have still not grasped the reality of our situation. Tell me, Mr. Stewart, how old would you estimate me to be?"

The wizard looked long and hard at his captor before answering, "When you've had a bad day I'd put you in your forties. In a good light you'd pass for early thirties."

Solovyev smiled. "I was born in 1866," he said. "I have spent most of my life pioneering research into bioelectricity – the energy which is created by and sustains the body. In the course of my work I discovered a means of supplementing my own energy from the reserves of others. I am able to sustain my vitality indefinitely. All I require are my machines and a supply of donors."

"And your two friends here, presumably," said Stewart.

The gracious smile didn't waver. "My two comrades have indeed been invaluable. They too have benefitted from the procedure. Aleksa Gorenya was born at the beginning of the twentieth century…"

"You ol' cradle-snatcher, you," said John B. drily. None of his captors responded.

The doctor continued unperturbed. "Comrade Gleb was born some thirty years later. Of the numerous assistants assigned to me by various agencies over time, these two showed the greatest aptitude for the tasks I required of them, and the greatest loyalty to me personally."

Solovyev turned his magnificent smile on Aleksa and Gleb, both of whom gave respectful nods of acknowledgement.

"Over the years the procedure has been progressively refined, particularly in the area of identifying optimum subjects for their bioelectricity, thanks in part to Comrade Yusupova's work. Not all men are created equal, contrary to some philosophies. Some possess much greater potential than others, and here I use the word 'potential' in the purely scientific sense. These men and women have become our preferred choice for the procedure. The energy derived from such people sustains us better and longer than that of, shall we say, lesser mortals."

John B. stared at the man who claimed to be over 140 years old. The Russian seemed to be serious.

"Most if not all of these individuals, however, seem blissfully ignorant of their potential and of what it may mean. This is to my – our – advantage obviously, as they are all the more easily obtained by my comrades and processed for our sustenance. You, Mr. Stewart, are a unique man even amongst the extraordinary. Your initial readings, the relative ease of your capture, and your subsequent resistance to the procedure are not congruent with each other. You have claimed repeatedly to not be offering conscious resistance and I am inclined to believe you. But can it really be possible that you do not know what you are?"

"Actually, I do. I'm bloody annoyed is what I am! I must be flypaper for freaks! You reckon that you three are a little cabal of electronic vampires? You really have put the 'mad' back into 'mad scientist'!" John B.'s studied air of restraint was finally cracking.

Aleksa jabbed a hypodermic needle into the wizard's arm before the exchange could go further. He turned an angry gaze on her even as his eyes began to glaze over.

The woman gave a little shrug and a smile that showed a lot of weariness, some satisfaction, a little confidence and no trace at all of sympathy. It was only to avoid having to deal with a stained tablecloth that she reached out and stopped Stewart from landing face-first in the soup.

*

The rhythmic mechanical sound was the pulse of the Rover's motor as it chugged along the road to school. The boy sat on the front bench seat, gazing out the window. Beside him was the car's driver – the woman he was still learning to routinely call 'Mum'.

"Are you alright, John? You've gone very quiet all of a sudden," she said.

"What? Oh – sorry. Sorry *Mum*," he replied, reinforcing the title for his own benefit. "I was just thinking."

"Oh aye? What about?" the woman asked, an edge of concern in her voice.

"Well, I know you said I'm a 'chosen child', but I was wondering – why did you choose *me*?"

Flora Stewart was silent for a moment. 'I don't really know' felt like it would have been a reasonably honest answer, but it seemed unkind. She thought for a bit, then measured her words carefully.

"Your Dad and I wanted a son. I must admit, we'd thought tae adopt someone a bit younger. But then the woman at the Home told us about you and how nobody knew anything about you – not even yourself. And we said tae each other, 'nae child should grow up thinking they're nae wanted by anyone'. So we met you, and talked to you. I said to Jock, 'he's a smart boy'. You were polite and we both liked you."

"And I liked you," replied the boy simply. "So now I'm a Stewart. That's good." He paused then said, "The Stewarts were royalty, weren't they?"

"Aye, a long time ago. Different spelling but the same clan right enough, if you go back far enough. Do you know about the Civil War?"

"The one in Britain? I've read a bit. We haven't been taught much at school – it's mostly Australian stuff there. I found a couple of books in the school library. I like history."

Flora glanced away from the road towards the boy she was learning to call her own and smiled. She approved of reading. It was often her only escape from a life that had denied her the opportunities she'd really wanted.

Family circumstance had taken her out of school early, and prevented her from pursuing further education later, even after she and her husband moved to Australia from 'the old country'. Sometimes she resented that, intuitively knowing she'd have been a good student, but now gloomily convinced that the chance had passed her by. But John was a clever boy, she realised. He would have the opportunities she didn't, whatever it took to make that happen.

Jock Stewart was of a similar view, fortunately. He was a tradesman who worked long hard hours, and he wanted the boy to have a future where he lived by his brains, not his hands. John would carry the ambitions of both his adoptive parents.

Flora's smile broadened a little as she said, "After I pick you up frae school this afternoon, we'll go to the library. We cannae afford tae buy you a lot of books, but we can go up there once a week and you can borrow to your heart's content."

Young John B. Stewart's enthusiasm was genuine. "That'd be great!" he said. "I really want to learn stuff!"

"*Stuff*, Doctor Solovyev? Should our paper to the Academy of Sciences not be a little more specific?"

Aleksa Yusupova had worked with the doctor for over twenty years, since the War, and she'd never before heard such a childlike tone in his voice.

Could something be going wrong with the procedure?

Solovyev shook his head sharply. "I am sorry, Comrade. A moment of… vagueness. Perhaps I am more tired than I had realised. It has passed. The paper for the Academy, yes – it is an inconvenience that we must bear."

They were the only two in the office. They could speak freely, knowing that their security chief Gleb was assiduous in ensuring that the recording devices his nominal superiors expected him to maintain were only operational when it suited Solovyev's purposes. The burly enforcer and the blonde scientist had come to an understanding some time earlier. The big man really was considerably smarter than he looked.

Aleksa glared angrily at the paper on the desk before her. There were only a few lines of her writing on the page. Clearly she had been struggling with what she could or should say.

"Comrade Doctor, why has Semichastnyi even spoken to the Academy of our work at all? The head of the KGB should not be sharing such information with anyone!" she snapped.

"He is young, and relatively new to his position. I think he senses that he truly knows little of what we do out here in our splendid isolation, and had hoped that someone in the Academy might enlighten him where the President would not."

The doctor leaned back in his comfortable chair and continued. "There is division between Khrushchev and the Academy, as you know."

"That could be dangerous for us."

Solovyev waved a lugubrious hand. "There is no reason that it should be so," he said. "Those who think themselves our masters in Moscow 'know' that we are researching the power of the mind, and ways of exploiting and controlling that power. We can write a report to reflect those objectives."

The woman looked unconvinced. She had been relieved when the purges that accompanied the transition from Stalin to Khrushchev had not swept them up, but was unsure that the doctor's meticulous planning and maneuvering could be so successful a second time.

Solovyev continued, "We are not the only State-sponsored researchers into the 'paranormal' you know. But the results we share are better than others. We have identified agents with potential beyond the ordinary – you have been a significant contributor to those results, comrade. We have brought out some of that potential for the benefit of Mother Russia. We have deleted certain memories of those deemed enemies of the State, and made them more tractable to involvement in the activities of the KGB. In short, we have done all that is expected of us by the miniscule few who know to expect anything at all. If some of our research subjects have failed to survive their testing, well, that is an unfortunate but sustainable loss as far as the Bureau is concerned. And a source of sustenance for us."

Aleksa nodded her understanding. "There are always more enemies of the state, and indeed, always more patriots willing to die in the belief of aiding their country. So, we shall tell the Academy enough to satisfy their 'professional interest' without provoking too much curiosity."

"Exactly. Our isolation from Moscow has made it easier for me to politely decline any invitations to active membership of the Academy, although I believe I am officially regarded as one of their number. As indeed are you, my dear."

She did not look entirely pleased by this news, having learned much appreciation of the clandestine existence of Konstantin Solovyev. "Khrushchev made it plain at July's plenum that he is opposed to the Academy, Comrade Doctor. Is it wise that we be seen to be aligned with it?"

"We are not," the doctor soothed. "If we are considered 'aligned' anywhere it is to the Presidency."

"I wonder if the KGB will try to prevail upon us to be involved in the inevitable shift of power," pondered his assistant.

"I doubt it. Managed correctly, this paper is actually an opportunity for us to insulate ourselves further. We emerge briefly from our den, as it were, give a reassuring wave that all is well, and withdraw to continue our efforts on 'their' behalf, with all parties believing that someone else has official responsibility for us. I stress, we are still theoretically ultimately answerable only to the Presidency. The office, not the incumbent man. Khrushchev may have some interest in the fringes of unconventional science, probably more so than in the conventional. But he has no understanding of either."

"I expect no better of his likely successor," said Aleksa disdainfully.

Solovyev shrugged. "Leonid Brezhnev is even more of a political animal. And we do not do politics, Aleksa – our first loyalty is to ourselves. If it becomes necessary to distance ourselves from the State then I possess appropriate resources, securely held in Switzerland. There are bankers there whose talent for secrecy matches my own. They are not successors to the French capitalists – they represent, I think, an evolution in their particular industry."

"Comrade Semichastnyi would not approve of the admiring tone of your observation," said Aleksa, smiling.

"Not officially, no. But I would expect a man in his position to take precautions of his own, just as I have always done. Now, let me assist you with this paper you find so vexing."

He gave Aleksa one of his perfect smiles.

Decades later, on the other side of the world, Aleksa was startled to receive an almost identical smile from the man lying unconscious on the laboratory table. She looked across the room to the doctor, regaining consciousness in his chair. He wore the same smile.

Yusupova shuddered. A chill ran down her spine as she left her console to remove the wires and skullcaps. Something in those matching expressions was deeply, deeply *wrong*.

.o0o.

25 FOR SAIL, FOR HIRE

"I'm sorry, but neither of you have sailed across the Strait before, and it's a notoriously tricky stretch of sea," said Wal, the now beleaguered proprietor of *Wal's World Of Watercraft*.

"Yes, we know. We knew that already, and you and someone in every other boat hire place out along the promontory have said the same thing."

"Well there you are then. Look, I'm sorry lady, but…"

Elizabeth drew herself up to her full height. She'd run out of patience. Fire flashed in her green eyes. Wilko knew the signs, winced, and prepared to jump in diplomatically.

"What I don't understand," she said, "is how you consider yourself to be a businessman."

With his afro hairstyle and thick moustache, Wal bore a more than passing resemblance to a 1970's porn star. But although he'd have said otherwise, he really wasn't good with a woman who showed real strength of character. So he looked more uncomfortable than offended as he opened his mouth to protest.

He didn't get a chance to speak before the feisty would-be customer continued.

"It's a quiet day, clearly. There's nobody else here lining up to give you money. We're not looking for favours, or a discount, or a deal – we just want to hire a boat. There's an S & S 34 sitting moored out there that would be ideal. I can hand you the cash. You can hold onto my credit card, if it will make you feel better."

Wal and Wilko both looked out at the thirty foot boat Elizabeth had mentioned. The vessel wasn't new, but she was well maintained.

Elizabeth opened her purse to extract her credit card. Business instincts caused Wal to look down. His eyes widened as he noticed her departmental business pass.

"Hey, wow!" he exclaimed. "I used to have one of those!"

Wilko and Elizabeth both looked at him in puzzlement.

"The pass card – I used to work in the Brisbane office!"

Elizabeth looked at him closely. "You weren't there at the same time as John Stewart, were you?"

"John B.? Purple t-shirt, hair like an unmade bed? Yeah – he left for Canberra about the same time as I chucked it in and headed south to sail and do boat stuff. He was one of the few people that said I wasn't crazy to quit, and I should follow my dreams."

Elizabeth nodded. "That'd be him."

The Tasmanian looked irked. "How does this stuff happen? He's a walking improbability field."

"Let's hope he *is* still walking," said Elizabeth a little curtly.

She and Wilko proceeded to explain to Wal the details of why they want ed to hire the boat, or at least, a sufficient outline of the story to enlist his sympathy.

At the end of the story the mustachioed man looked solemn.

"The *Helen Back* is yours," he said, gesturing out of the office towards the moored S & S 34. "Just bring her back in one piece. And bring John B. with her too, eh?"

"That's the plan," said Elizabeth.

Wal took them aboard the *Helen Back* and gave them a thorough briefing on her foibles and features. He was clearly fond of the vessel.

"27 horsepower engine, Bermuda rig with an overlapping headsail. Did you know Ted Heath - the British Prime Minister - won the 1969 Sydney to Hobart with one of these? The *Morning Cloud*."

"She's one of a fine breed," said Wilko, patting *Helen*'s fiberglass side affectionately.

"Yeah, they've got a long history of being super seaworthy. There have been a few circumnavigations of the planet in S & S 34s y'know. Some of them single handed."

"Not quite as far as we aim to go, but it's an encouraging thing to hear," said Elizabeth.

"Right enough," Wal agreed. "I've put as many safety features as I can in her, but. I don't know if you've seen one of these – it's the latest model."

Wal pointed to a bright orange hard plastic object prominently positioned on the teak deck at the aft of the boat. It looked like a cross between a walkie-talkie and a heavy-duty torch.

"That's an EPIRB – Emergency Position Indicating Response Beacon," he explained. "Brand new and guaranteed. Very handy if your boat breaks down in the middle of open sea."

Wilko's smile was thin. "Let's try not to need it then," he said.

.o0o.

26 CROSSING OVER

It had been simply a bloody rotten night of trying to sleep, John B. thought to himself.

He lay on his bed, gazing at the portrait on the wall.

"Were you a cavalryman?" he asked the distinguished painted figure. "Is that what I should wish for? Someone to come riding to my rescue?"

The wizard stared at the back of the locked door, and considered the three individuals who lived and worked on the other side of it.

"I think not," he replied to himself. "These jokers are the very bloody image of mad, bad and dangerous to know. I don't want anyone else to have to deal with them. That should be my wish – whatever happens to me, they don't use this damned 'procedure' on anyone else. Ever again."

To Stewart's surprise there was a polite knock on the door. 'Has to be Mr. Perfect,' he thought. "Come in," he said aloud.

As expected, it was indeed Doctor Solo who entered the room. The blonde man sat on the end of the bed. He looked tired.

"Good morning Mr. Stewart. We will be conducting the procedure again shortly. I could politely say 'I am sorry', but you and I both know that is not true," he said.

"If 'sorry' means regretting that it happens, I certainly am," replied the prisoner.

In spite of himself, Solovyev smiled. "A semantic somersault. Very good. In the same sense, I too am truly sorry. I would rather this had been over and done with days ago. But I will persist, and you will succumb."

John B. didn't change his expression of studied indifference. "One definition of insanity is to repeat the same actions and expect a different result."

"Ah, but they are not the same actions. With every iteration Aleksa and I change the parameters. Refine the settings of our machines. Increase the pressure on your formidable resistance. I feel that I am… learning more about you, although it remains indistinct. You have never been a soldier?"

After a pause, Stewart replied, "Not that I can remember off-hand."

"It is not training then. Although, you need not have been aware of it. I have performed such manipulations myself."

"I know."

The Russian looked at him in surprise.

"I don't know what there is of *me* stuck in *your* head, but one of the reasons I can't sleep is because of flashes of things that can only be from you," continued Stewart. "I've no idea how you can sleep with that history."

Disconcerted, the doctor falteringly replied, "I have done what I had to."

"Following orders, I see. A popular defence, that. It saves taking responsibility. So you weren't fighting for 'the cause'. Come on, tell me – what did you believe in?"

"Surviving. Just as I do now. I make no apologies, Mr. Stewart. I was not 'following orders'. My first priority is, was, and always shall be, myself."

"I get that. Maybe more than I'd like to admit. But there's a lot to be said for looking outside of yourself. For one thing, others are more inclined to look out for you."

"Self sufficiency, Mr. Stewart, self sufficiency. Relying on others is a recipe for disappointment," said Solovyev, unconsciously putting into perspective his relationship with Aleksa and Gleb – still cautious after all the years.

"Reliance isn't the same as trust, far less *care*. I don't know if you've lost that, or never even had it to begin with."

The Russian shrugged. "Does it matter?" he said as he jabbed a needle into Stewart's leg. "I will have your power, John Stewart, however hard you resist."

"John *B.* Stewart," insisted the wizard doggedly, even as the room spun into darkness.

*

The wizard had a flickering of consciousness as he lay on the table, wires already embedded in his skull. He saw Solovyev being helped into his chair by Aleksa before she applied the doctor's own skullcap.

'Looks like he's not doing too well either,' he mused. 'Don't know quite what it is that I'm doing, but I hope I can outlast him. I don't feel like I've got much left…'

As he lapsed back into darkness he heard, again, the throb of the machines. Aleksa had again recalibrated them and the sensation had gone beyond a vague throb to an insistent pounding.

Thud. Thud. Thud. As relentless and methodical as a machine himself, Gleb moved the nail gun along the wall, attaching the brace that would hold some of the soon-to-be-reassembled equipment.

"I know that we are only fifty miles or so from the mainland, but this feels more remote than the installation in the tundra where we first met. I think perhaps I am not comfortable with livink on an island," complained the other 'assistant' as she unwrapped electrical equipment from its insulated wrapping.

"Then you will have to learn, dear Aleksa. Think of it as 'splendid isolation'. It is the most secure location I could find in which we can continue our work unhindered," Solovyev replied patiently as he uncoiled a length of electrical cable.

"But Australia? The far side of the Earth? Could you not have found somethink nearer – Eastern Europe perhaps? A government there would have supported us surely," she persisted.

The doctor shook his head. "Not for long, I think. Times are changing comrade, as they inevitably do. To survive, we change with them. I learned this long ago. We have had to learn to accommodate this *glas-nost*."

Without turning his head Gleb grunted contemptuously. "Gorbachev is a fool. Russian power derives from central authority, not 'open government' nonsense. Already the Soviet Union begins to disintegrate. It needs a strong leader to impose his will."

"And that may well happen in time, comrade. I see these changes, these shifts in power, and I move with them to my best advantage. I see the gates of secrecy being opened, our walls being torn down. The true nature of our work has been well hidden, even from the *apparatchiks* of our government, but I could foresee that not remaining so."

Aleksa sighed in agreement. "There are those who would not approve of our methods."

"*Da*, and others who would care less about our methods than about appropriating the results for themselves," said the doctor. "That unpleasant young man who is trying to make a name for himself in the KGB – he shows no scruples…"

"He would make a good leader, then," observed Gleb.

"Perhaps. He would not be the first of his type. But as I said a long time ago, we are not in the business of politics. The Solovyev Institute operated, however covertly, under the auspices of the State only so far as it was of mutual benefit. That situation was changing rapidly. I judged that the time was right to move on."

"But such a move!"

"Yes Aleksa, you have made your point," Solovyev replied, some asperity betrayed in his voice. "The resources that I could trust, even within the deepest reaches of the KGB, even among our own former 'patients', were scant. It was all that I could do to find someone within the operations of the Australian government who could be manipulated into unobtrusively transferring this piece of 'Crown Land' to us, complete with this 'Ranger's accommodation' for us to claim. This ample storage basement will house our equipment perfectly, and our own rather special generators will provide a more than generous supply of power. We will operate without any risk of interference from any government, anywhere. If the name of the Solovyev Institute should henceforth ever attract attention in Moscow we will not be found. It will be as if we were never there. So we survive, and our work goes on."

"But to what end now?" Aleksa insisted, in a last flourish of disillusionment.

"To *our* benefit, not to the benefit of the State – *any* state, and this is as it should ever be. Certainly we do not work to an *end*," said Solo, smiling at his own small joke.

  Almost in unison Yusupova and Skripitsyn replied, "Yes, Comrade Doctor."

"Just 'Doctor' will do," he said lugubriously. "We are in a new country, embarking on a new life. Yes, I have a shipping container full of the com forts and reminders of home due to arrive soon, but for the most part we can dispense with the old restrictions. It will be easy – you shall see." His smile broadened. "I have already forgotten so much of my past!"

The Matron frowned at the boy.

"I fail to understand why you would sound so proud of such a thing. Running away from home is quite bad enough, and I am willing to accept that some dire circumstance may have caused you to suppress certain memories. But to speak as though you were pleased, even delighted to have no recollection at all of your past – that, young man, I will not countenance."

"No ma'am. I'm sorry, ma'am. I didn't mean to sound pleased."

"Hmph. Very well – apology accepted. John, you must understand that you are in a very difficult situation. You were found by the police, wandering the streets alone with virtually no belongings beyond the clothes that even now you stand up in. Jeans, sandshoes, and what is frankly a rather tattered purple t-shirt that is too small for you. No identification, other than the name "John B." scribbled on the neck of your shirt. There wasn't even a sign of accident or injury."

The Matron's expression softened as she continued, "You told the police you couldn't remember anything of who you were or how you got there. Is this still the case?"

"Yes ma'am. Which is to say, *no* ma'am. I can't remember a thing."

"You've got no idea what the 'B' stands for?"

"No ma'am. Bewildered, maybe?"

She smiled and drummed her fingers on her desk.

"You're a bright lad, at least. I know much older children who wouldn't even have the word 'bewildered' in their vocabulary. Well, now you're here. The D'Oliviera Home for Orphaned Children will be your home until and unless we are able to identify your parents. You may be put up for adoption, depending on the Court's discretion, but I should warn you that the likelihood of any good family taking on a child of such unknown, dubious origin and history is remote."

"Yes ma'am. I understand."

"Do you even know how old you are, John?"

"No, ma'am."

"Alright. You look about the right size for a ten year old, so that's what I shall consider you to be. For official purposes, until evidence to the contrary appears, today, your date of admission to the Orphanage, will be taken to be your tenth birthday."

The boy smiled. "So this is my birthday, ma'am?"

"Yes John."

"May I request a present, please?" He chose his words carefully. His recent experience with the policemen who'd picked him up off the street had been a swift and salient lesson in the importance of being polite to those who considered themselves authority figures.

The diplomatic approach worked.

The Matron smiled back at him and replied, "You may request. I cannot guarantee that you shall receive what you ask for, though.”

“May I have a new shirt please ma’am? A purple one if that’s possible.”

She nodded. “It was already my intention that you would get a small wardrobe from our store of donated clothes. If there is a purple shirt there in your size, you may have it.”

“Thank you ma’am!”

“I might ask, though – is there a particular reason for purple? Some memory?”

The boy looked thoughtful.

“No ma’am. I don’t think so. I think it’s just… my colour.”

The Matron’s smile wavered as she wondered what were the origins of the enigma that was mysterious little John B.

As if reading her thoughts, John B.’s brow creased too. He was wondering the same thing.

“Not… satisfactory… at all.” Solovyev’s voice was barely more than a grunt as he regained consciousness.

Aleksa shook her head in bafflement and said, “With the settinks I am usink you should be drawing energy from him like blood into a syringe. But you derive no benefit?”

“Barely. A light refreshment perhaps, but barely more than what I find I am expending of myself. There are – other things that I am drawing from him, but not the energy that I desire. That I *need*. I still do not know if his resistance is deliberate or instinctive. But I *will* overcome it! I wish that the means to do so *will* present itself to me!"

As she removed the wires from the blonde scalp, Agony Aleksa pondered at Doctor Solo's unusual, uncharacteristic choice of words.

.oOo.

It hadn't been an easy morning for Wilko and Elizabeth.

They'd had to plough the *Helen Back* into a constant headwind. Green water had crashed across her deck almost since their departure.

Wilko had initially been surprised at Elizabeth's seamanship.

"Hey, you're a natural at this, aren't you?" he'd said.

"Always been keen," she'd replied with a grimace as *Helen* pitched under her. "Just a matter of experience."

Experience was something they'd certainly gotten in a hurry. It wasn't a storm – the sky was reasonably clear. It was just Bass Strait's normal surly character, as the Tasmanian described it.

At one point Wilko looked aft and swallowed nervously.

"I don't like the company we're keeping," he said.

In the water behind them several dark dorsal fins were breaking the surface.

"They're not dolphins, are they?" asked Elizabeth.

"Don't think so. I'd rather not fall in the water and find out the hard way."

"Fair enough. Let's try not to sink the boat then, hey?" she said mildly.

Wilko looked back, again, and shuddered. "Agreed."

They were sailing into a bumpy and seemingly empty grey horizon when

Wilko looked up from the waterproof chart that Wal had provided them with.

"Got to be over that way," he said, pointing to the south-east.

Now the sun was high in the sky. A particularly heavy swell lifted the *Helen* even higher than usual. A small dark green lump briefly became visible between the choppy waves, still some distance away.

"Land ho!" called Elizabeth with a grin.

It wasn't long before they managed to draw their monohulled vessel into the shelter of a small cove.

"I think we're in the right place," said Elizabeth. She pointed to a boat tied up at a small pier. It was a similar size to the *Helen Back*, but considerably newer.

They carefully berthed on the opposite side of the small pier from the other vessel. It was with more relief than caution that they clambered up onto the wooden platform.

Their concentration was fixed on securing the rope tying the *Helen Back* to the dock. So they didn't see Gleb emerge from the track through the bushes fringing the area around their landing point. The ex-KGB enforcer had been on the way to the pier to distract himself with some maintenance, and purely by chance had spotted their boat as they approached Mundara.

Visitors were neither common, nor welcome. Doctor Solovyev preferred that they be sent on their way as quickly and quietly as possible with polite but firm warnings about Private Property. The doctor didn't consider it prudent to have them simply disappear into his basement lab as 'fodder' for the procedure. You couldn't know who might miss them or start asking awkward questions. That was why the 'protocol' of Aleksa's expeditions to the mainland had been developed.

On this day, however, Gleb was not in the mood to be prudent. He was tired. His body badly needed the reinvigoration that Dr. Solo's procedure provided. He was bigger than the other two – he needed to be 'fed' more often, he reasoned. Stewart's resistance and Solovyev's obstinacy had made him even more aggressive than usual.

As he quietly stalked towards the pier, he drew his trusty and trusted Makarov pistol from the concealed holster he still routinely wore. Old habits died hard, and the semi-automatic service handgun had been a part of Skripitsyn's life since the 1950's.

"You are not welcome here. Leave now!" he barked.

Elizabeth and Wilko jumped in surprise. The Tasmanian lost his balance and stumbled, landing heavily back down on the timber deck of their boat.

The brunette stood and stared into the ugly face. 'We've found our man alright,' she thought to herself.

"No," she replied. "I don't think we will. This is Mundara, right?"

The greasy haired man frowned. There was something disconcerting about the woman's confident green-eyed gaze, but he was too weary and too angry to pay heed to any subconscious warnings.

"*Da*. It is private property. I give you one warning, and that is all. Get back on your boat and go away now."

"No," Elizabeth repeated. "I think that there's someone here we want to see."

"There is no-one here of any consequence to you," snarled Gleb, flicking the barrel of the pistol towards the *Helen Back* to suggest that the woman should get back aboard.

Wilko had struggled back to his feet, and was looking at the Makarov with concern. He didn't like guns, and he'd seen far too many of them recently. He looked up and recognised the pistol's wielder. Even through the veil of Agony Aleksa's hypnotism, Gleb's face was not readily forgotten, however much you might want to.

"You're that guy from the pub…" he began, still a little unsteady from the fall.

Gleb didn't acknowledge the smaller man. "I am most willing to shoot you both," he said.

"Well, I am not willing to leave this lump of rock without the answers I want, so you'll probably just have to," Elizabeth answered evenly.

"As you wish," said Gleb. "There are eight bullets in this gun. I will need only two to kill you both. Your boat will burn and you will be presumed to have been lost at sea."

"You have it all worked out, eh? Done this before, have you?" asked the brunette in a casual tone.

Gleb almost smiled. Solovyev did not know quite everything that went on around the shore of the island.

"*Da*," said the ugly man.

"Ah… Elizabeth?" came a worried voice from the deck of the *Helen Back*.

"Quiet, Wilko. So, if you're going to shoot me, can I have a last cigarette?"

Her erstwhile crewmate looked puzzled. "I thought you'd given up?" he
ventured.

"Will you shut up, please Wilko? Last smoke."

"*Da*. Why not?" The happy prospect of killing someone made Skripitsyn
almost magnanimous.

Elizabeth took a lighter out of the bag she'd taken off the boat, and then
rummaged for a bit.

"There's a few left in here somewhere, in my last packet…" she said,
distractedly.

"Your last packet, *da*. Last ever," said Gleb, in what was for him an at-
tempt at wit. He stepped closer, raising the pistol to align with Elizabeth's
heart.

Suddenly she pulled an aerosol can of hairspray from the bag, flicked the
lighter and sent a jet of flame into the Russian's gun hand.

There was an incongruous high-pitched squeal from the former enforcer
as he jumped back and dropped the weapon.

"Now Wilko, quick! Do something!" she cried.

"What? Me?!? He's twice my size! What do you expect…"

Wilko had never actually hit anyone in his life, even when he'd been a Sunday morning C-grade footballer. That thought rapidly triggered another thought. He grabbed the EPIRB from the deck and hurled it like the throw-ins he'd taken on soccer fields around Hobart. At just over two metres his accuracy was impeccable – a half-kilo of electrical equipment and hard plastic casing thudded hard into the Russian's face.

Stunned, Gleb fell backwards into the water.

Elizabeth helped Wilko up onto the pier and gave him a quick hug.

"Good shot mate – well done," she said.

Wilko looked at the hairspray she was casually putting back in her bag. "Remind me never to get you mad at me," he said quietly as he picked up the Emergency Beacon to return it to the *Helen Back*.

"Right," Elizabeth replied with a grin.

"Should we check on him?" asked Wilko from the deck of their boat, pointing to the other side of the pier.

"We've got more important priorities, haven't we? Oh alright."

With some irritated reluctance she looked down into the water.

"Yeah, he's floating face up," she reported.

Wilko sighed considerable relief. Repellant as Gleb was, and despite the ugly man's threats branding him as a probable psychopath, the Tasmanian didn't want a death on his conscience.

Elizabeth indicated the path through the trees and said, "Looks like that's where he came from. Let's go find John, eh?"

'If he's here alive,' was Wilko's unspoken thought as he considered Gleb's pistol.

It wasn't a long walk. The path was easy enough with the only potential hazards being the occasional mutton bird burrow to break an unwary ankle. The nests were untenanted, Gleb having long since used their former residents as goulash ingredients.

Mundara was quite a lush little island. The plants were well watered by the Strait's weather. That meant that Solovyev's house was well hidden until you turned the final corner of the path and it suddenly revealed itself.

Elizabeth and Wilko stopped short at their first sight of it. A single storey timber structure it was less incongruous than, say, a gothic manor would have been. Any sort of house would frankly have seemed out of place on the isolated island. But seemingly grafted onto an otherwise plain building were touches of opulence, like real French windows and elegant shutters that would have indicated wealth in any setting.

Cautiously, the pair approached the house. The door stood a little ajar. Gleb hadn't bothered to close it behind him knowing that the island had no wildlife likely to go in, and sanguine about their prisoner attempting to escape. He would welcome the excuse to kill the hairy man.

Elizabeth pushed the door further open.

"Careful!" said Wilko in an urgent whisper. "That woman's around somewhere and I'll bet she's as dangerous as her gruesome pal."

"Probably worse," agreed Elizabeth. "I've got this far and I'm not stop ping now."

Wilko shook his head, sighed to himself and quietly followed her into the house.

Uncomfortably aware of the sound of their footsteps on the polished wooden floor they started checking rooms on either side of the corridor.

There were dishes stacked neatly in the drainer beside the kitchen sink. The benches and stove top were clear.

A well-decorated parlour was clearly unoccupied. A large ornate samovar on the mantlepiece over the fireplace gave mute testimony to the owner's Eastern European origins. The crystal glassware beside it indicated wealth, and plenty of it. A hearth cut from a single stone showed signs of regular use. Mundara could get cold, obviously.

Two bedrooms were remarkably similar in the aristocratic style of their furnishing. There was nothing to clearly indicate the gender of either occupant, since the two intruders stopped short of rifling wardrobes or drawers.

There were two bathrooms, both with fine brass fittings. They didn't bother to check the cabinets in either.

Then they found a third bedroom, Spartan and untidy. A tub of hair oil and a box of 9mm ammunition on the dresser made it clear who lived in the room.

Wilko jerked a thumb at the other bedrooms they'd just seen.

"Why does she need two rooms?" he whispered.

"Greedy? She uses a different room for weekends? Maybe there's more than one of her? Does it matter?" The tension showed in Elizabeth's quiet voice.

As Wilko went to enter the lounge room Elizabeth tried the door of the room opposite.

"It's locked," she called softly over her shoulder.

The Tasmanian turned and stood at her shoulder as she rattled the door handle.

"You've got the key, haven't you? Let yourself in!" came a tired, irritated but familiar voice from inside the room.

"John! Is that you?" exclaimed Elizabeth, unable to keep her voice down in her excitement.

There was a moment's pause before the same voice, now perplexed, replied, "Q? What the…?"

"Wilko's with me. Hang on while we get this door open. I'm so glad you're alive! Any idea where the key to this door is?"

"That would be this one," said a smooth voice behind them.

Wilko spun but Elizabeth controlled herself, turning slowly and carefully.

Just inside the doorway of the lounge room stood two blondes. The man who had just spoken had a white coat over one arm and held a small bunch of keys in his outstretched hand. Elizabeth resisted returning his smile – it was almost impossibly perfect.

At his side was a blonde woman, still wearing her lab coat and pointing a small gun at the two intruders. Even without make-up, the Tasmanian recognised her striking features.

"I'd have sworn that room was empty. Hello Aleksa," he said with commendable calm.

"Hello Weelko," she replied evenly. "Do not move. This weapon is a PSM pistol. It may look small but its bullets can penetrate 55 layers of Kevlar, so you can be assured of it doink considerable damage to your body. I am surprised to see you here."

Wilko held his nerve and answered casually, "I'm a little surprised myself, to be honest."

"Weelko, is it? Notwithstanding your uninvited presence in my home, courtesy obliges me to say 'Welcome to Mundara'. My name is Doctor Konstantin Solovyev." The doctor's smile was dazzling if not actually sincere.

The man at the wrong end of the gun swallowed but kept his voice steady as he said, "It's Wilko, actually. Your lady friend's pronunciation is a bit off."

"My apologies, Mr. Wilko. I note that *your* lady friend has not said anything," said Solovyev.

Elizabeth looked at the two blondes. The man seemed more self-assured than threatening, although his eyes were cold. The woman with the gun, on the other hand, had a more obvious air of menace about her.

"What's to say? John's alive. That's good. You've appeared out of nowhere in an empty room, pointing a gun at us. Not so good. Now what?"

"Now I kill you both, I think," answered Aleksa.

Doctor Solo laid a hand on her gun arm, not so heavily as to affect her
aim, and said, "No, Aleksa, I think not. Mr. Stewart clearly means a great
deal to these two. It is to hope that they mean as much to him."

Through the locked door of his room, John B. heard every word of the
exchange, and was not cheered by it.

'I don't like where this is going,' he thought.

There was a crash that reverberated down the corridor as the front door
was kicked open. Leaving a trail of water on the polished hall floor, Gleb
stormed towards Elizabeth and Wilko. There was still blood welling from
the bridge of his nose.

"With my bare hands I kill them! Even with this one!" he shouted, bran-
dishing the hand that was already showing where the burn scars would be.

Solo stepped into the corridor, blocking the big man's way.

"Gleb! No! Not now!" he said firmly.

The former security man stopped, breathing heavily as he said, "These
two, they will die! The woman burned me. The little man broke my face.
They left me to drown…"

In his room John B. raised his eyebrows. There were facets of Q and
Wilko he hadn't seen, obviously. But an angry Skripitsyn could only
make matters worse.

"I wish that I can keep them safe," he muttered, then called out, "Solo! Keep your gorilla on a leash!"

The magnificent smile that had disappeared when confronting the angry Gleb returned.

"Mr. Stewart, I will happily restrain my eager associate…"

The ugly man glowered but the doctor held up a warning hand as he continued, "I do, of course, expect your co-operation in return."

Suspicion, distrust and puzzlement were all in Elizabeth's eyes. "John – what's going on?" she asked.

"I'm not sure I can give you a clear answer - sorry, pretty lady," came the voice through the door.

The doctor's expression didn't change but he did note the term of affection.

"I am going to unlock your door, Mr. Stewart. You will join us in the parlour. No foolish heroics please. I assure you that the only possible consequences are either that Aleksa will shoot your friends or Gleb will break their necks. Possibly both."

The colour had drained from Wilko's face. The handsome young blonde bloke was clearly serious.

Growling, Gleb led the way to the parlour.

Aleksa's concentration was fully focused on her small slim pistol as she followed the new prisoners, so she failed to notice the faint vibration and flashing red light from the small device in her lab coat pocket. It was the same device that Stewart and Wilko had noticed her using in *The Capital*.

Gleb stood in the doorway and shoved his two assailants into the room. As Aleksa covered them with her deadly little PSM the ugly man tied up the new captives hand and foot with a polypropylene rope he'd fetched from the kitchen. He bound them back to back then kicked their feet out from under them.

They fell heavily to the floor beside the hearth just as Solovyev walked into the room, a hand on Stewart's shoulder.

"Gleb!" rapped the doctor. "That will do! Our new guests are important to Mr. Stewart, and thus to us."

"To you," the big man growled.

Solovyev glared at his long-time ally. The smile had disappeared, and his face creased into an intense look of warning. In a low voice Solo said, "*U meenya galavnya bol' apasni*, Gleb."

"The doctor has a dangerous headache," observed Stewart, his own voice reflecting his captor's threatening tone. Gleb flashed a quick look of angry surprise at the wizard before looking back at Solovyev.

It was a contest of wills which could only ever have one result. The enforcer curled his lip but mumbled, "As you say, Comrade Doctor."

Tied as they were, the new captives couldn't compare the puzzled expressions they both wore. Neither of them had any idea that John B. was any sort of linguist. He'd never shown evidence of it in their experience. They vaguely knew he had an Arts degree, but there had never been men tion of his majoring in Languages. It wasn't relevant at work, and hadn't come up socially. In Canberra Stewart didn't talk much about his past.

The wizard surveyed the room. He was still coming to terms with the unexpected arrival of Q and Wilko, worrying about his earlier musings about 'the cavalry' arriving. He folded his arms and did his best to look casual. "So – here we all are then," he said.

.o0o.

28 ALL IN THIS TOGETHER

Gleb loomed in the doorway of the parlour. He was looking about the room, casting unpleasant looks at every occupant.

There was resentment aimed at the doctor. Skripitsyn felt badly in need of the restorative effects of the Procedure, and he was fed up with what he regarded as his mentor's obsession with their most recent subject.

There was intense dislike and resentment of John B. Stewart. What was so special about him? He should be just another victim, drained and discarded. He was too ready to insult his betters, and Dr. Solo was at fault for not allowing him to be suitably punished.

There was irritated jealousy of Aleksa – simply of the fact that she still possessed her slim little PSM pistol. He hadn't been able to find his own beloved Makarov – Wilko had in fact impulsively picked it up and flung it as far as he could out to sea.

It was for the two new prisoners that he felt the most intense of emotions. Anger - hate even. He had been injured, but worse, humiliated. By a little man and a mere woman. What he wanted was simple: revenge. He longed to make it as brutal as possible. He would make them suffer before he killed them.

Sitting comfortably in his chair, Solovyev watched the expressions on his ugly enforcer's face as he gazed about. Gleb could never have been a successful poker player.

The doctor directed a languid hand towards the figure in the doorway. "My dear guests, I invite you all to study the face of my esteemed comrade," he said.

"Cruel and unusual treatment, that is," observed John B.

"You really should not provoke him further, Mr. Stewart. He is clearly not happy, and that does not bode well for your friends as it is. Consider them hostages to your good behavior. Inflaming Gleb's already volatile temper will only make their lot worse if you do not fully co-operate in our next session."

The wizard met the doctor's gaze squarely and said, "It's news to me that I wasn't co-operating. I didn't think I'd had the option of putting up much of a fight."

Solovyov smiled his dazzling smile. "You are too modest. Your mental defences have been remarkably formidable. You have an extraordinary mind, which is of course to be expected…"

"Him?!? Now I *know* you're mad!" exclaimed Wilko.

The scientist raised amused eyebrows. 'Clearly', he thought, 'this Stewart has not shared his past with his friends. I would not either. But is it possible… could he really *not* know what he is?'

"You greatly underestimate your colleague, Mr. Wilko. Or perhaps you know better and seek to mislead me. No matter," the blonde Russian purred. "Mr. Stewart, you will relax those defences. What you have, I will possess. Or I will allow Gleb to take his considerable aggravation out on your friends."

"He will be enjoyink that, I think," said Aleksa with a smile that had no trace of warmth in it.

Even through his fear, a part of Wilko's mind was puzzling over the doctor's comments. The same was true of Elizabeth, although there were other emotions also swirling in her head.

John B. looked across at the two of them, bound back to back sitting on the floor, then at the looming, still damp but still greasy Gleb. The enforcer looked like he was already mentally compiling a list of ways to painfully remove body parts without immediately killing his victims.

The wizard shook his head. "Look, to save them I wish I *could* let you have it – even a part of whatever it is you're trying to – extract."

"*Spaceeba.* We shall make another try then, shall we? Miss Yusupova – you know what to do. Gleb, do not damage our guests. I am very serious – restrain yourself, for now at least. If Stewart is not sufficiently co-operative I want him to be able to see you work your ministrations on them."

The unspoken thought behind Solovyov's courteous reply was, 'Of course, presuming that the procedure works correctly this time, he will be past seeing or caring about anything or anyone'.

Elizabeth was facing away from John B., but got an excellent view of Aleksa walking across the room flicking the tip of a hypodermic needle, the PSM back in her coat pocket.

"What are you going to do to him?" she shouted as she tried to turn, succeeding only in toppling both herself and Wilko sideways so that now neither could see what was going on.

John B. adopted what he hoped was his most soothing and reassuring voice as he said, "It's okay Q – it's a muscle relaxant. I'm getting used to this."

The last sentence completely undid any slim chance there might have been of putting Q's mind at ease. The wizard realised this when he saw her body tense further.

"It's okay! I'll be okay. I've managed so far," he tried to reassure her as the needle went into his arm.

The familiar sense of sinking into something damp and dense started to overcome the wizard. As his vision blurred he saw Gleb standing over his friends.

"Struggle, hairy man. I look forward to hurting these two," growled Skripitsyn.

"I wish you luck with that, pal," mumbled the wizard. "The worst kind of luck."

.o0o.

29 POKING THE BEAR

Gleb had carried the unconscious wizard out of the parlour and into the lounge room, out of the line of sight of either Elizabeth or Wilko.

Solo gave something like a gracious bow to the two bound captives. "With Mr. Stewart in a more – tractable – frame of mind, given his concern for your welfare, I believe I shall step my equipment up to new levels. I expect remarkable results," he said with his usual smile.

Aleksa nodded and said, "As you deserve, Doctor."

The two Russians waited for their ugly compatriot to return from the basement. He was back within a few minutes.

"Miss Yusupova and I must take our leave for some time," the doctor told the bound pair smoothly. "Meanwhile you shall be in Gleb's hands." He turned to the enforcer and the smile vanished. "I do *not* mean that literally. I stress again, my old comrade, our hostages are not to be damaged. I do not want their value compromised, do you understand?"

"*Da*, Comrade Doctor," was the obviously reluctant reply.

The blonde man rested a hand on his comrade's shoulder. "Good," he said. "When I return we will… consider the situation."

The men exchanged knowing looks. The expression that Aleksa turned on the prisoners had a definite air of finality. Head held high, she followed Solovyev out of the parlour.

The sound of their footsteps on the wooden floor echoed down the corridor. Gleb stood listening wordlessly for a few minutes. Then he stalked out of the parlour. Unseen by anyone, he walked into the lounge room and checked that the unobtrusive trapdoor in the polished floor was securely closed. He didn't expect that anything that happened up here would distract the doctor or Aleksa, but it was better to be cautious than invite Solovyev's displeasure.

In his absence, the two prisoners struggled unsuccessfully against their ropes.

"Any ideas?" whispered Wilko, unsure of how close their guard may be.

"Maybe," Elizabeth answered, just as softly. "I'll try something. Trust me, okay?"

Before he could make a reply alluding to their recent experience on the pier, their watchman returned. The big man's simmering rage was palpable.

"I am having trouble deciding," announced Gleb, settling into an armchair. "Should I break your girlfriend first, or make her watch while I break you?"

"She's not my girlfriend!" exclaimed Wilko.

His objection was rapidly followed by Elizabeth's own loud protest, "I'm *nobody's* girlfriend!"

"Hah! I am not surprised, with your attitude!" said the Russian with a barking sound that was his version of a laugh.

"Oh, and you're clearly such an expert on women," she snapped back sharply. "With your looks I'm sure you've had a lot of girlfriends. I doubt that any of them walked on less than four legs, mind you."

"Shut your mouth, bitch!"

"Elizabeth, why the hell are you provoking him?" demanded Wilko, in a whisper.

"Angry men are careless men I've found," was the equally quiet reply.

Wilko rolled his eyes. "Careless maybe, but violent too!" he warned.

"Well yes, I've noticed that, too," she admitted, but carried on regardless. "You can't scare me Glob – your boss said no damage to us, and I don't reckon you're game to ever stand up to him, are you?"

The burly former agent slowly rose from his chair and walked over to where the two friends lay. With considerable deliberation he kicked Elizabeth.

Smiling down at her Gleb said, "I have many years knowledge of where to hurt you and leave no mark."

Wincing back the pain Q retorted, "So you're afraid to let him *see* your little act of defiance, are you? You really don't have a backbone, do you Glob?"

Skripitsyn's smile, unpleasant as it was, disappeared. "I owe Doctor Solovyov everything," he snarled. "It is thanks to him I am what I am today. He made me…"

Elizabeth interrupted, "You can't imagine he's proud of that, can you?

What did he use? Spare parts? Sweepings from the abattoir floor?"

The big man growled, "I was about to say, Comrade Doctor made me immortal. A pity nobody has done the same for you. Pity for you, eh?"

Gleb drew his right foot back a long way, aiming a kick which might not leave a mark but would do a lot of internal damage.

Suddenly Elizabeth rolled, using her own body as a pivot point to swing Wilko around. The small man's flailing knees cracked into Gleb's left leg.

Skripitsyn crashed to the floor, instinctively grabbing at the mantlepiece as he fell. The wooden shelf ripped from the wall. The heavy samovar landed on Gleb's right temple just as his left temple struck the stone edge of the fireplace. The ornate glasses smashed as they landed, some of them bouncing off the enforcer even as he died.

"Now that sounded like bad luck for him," observed Q calmly as she tried to roll back to a position where she could see the damage.

Wilko failed to repress a shudder. "He was wrong about being immortal."

Elizabeth grunted in pain as her movement sparked sharp pain where Gleb's boot had struck.

"Don't expect me to be sorry," she said. "I heard glass break. Any decent sized bits land near you?"

"Yeah. If we can move a bit this way… ow!"

The attempts to bounce and roll in the direction Wilko had indicated suddenly stopped.

"Are you okay? Can you reach the glass?" she asked.

"I'm sitting on some of it!"

"Ooh – sorry!"

The next set of movements was rather more careful. They managed to maneuver themselves into a position whereby Wilko could grasp a lengthy shard, and with only several lacerations to all four wrists eventually slice through their bonds.

Untying their ankles they gingerly got to their feet.

"Now," said Elizabeth decisively, "I think we better look for John."

"Yeah. This isn't a room I want to hang around in."

Wilko couldn't suppress a shudder as he stepped over Gleb's corpse. Not looking down, he didn't see the Russian's skin starting to fold in on itself as years of bio-electrically achieved revivification began to fall away.

Skripitsyn wasn't a pretty sight to begin with. This was only making matters worse. Don't imagine it – move on.

.oOo.

30 CROSS YOUR HEART AND HOPE TO…

There'd been a repetitive, rhythmic sound. It seemed familiar. Waking up was proving to be difficult – if this actually was 'waking up'. He realised he wasn't sure.

John B. was lying on a beach. He didn't know where. The sand was white and gritty. There were… rocks? A cliff maybe, in the distance. It was hard to focus.

The rhythmic noise he heard – it was a small surf, breaking well off shore. Water lapped at his feet, little more than warm ripples. The sky… there was something funny about the sky. It was empty.

Empty of birds. Empty of clouds. Empty of – blue. It was like the colour of the sand reflected in old glass.

Stewart tried to stir but his arms and legs didn't seem inclined to cooperate. He was lying on his right side. With effort he managed to lift his head. There was someone walking along the beach.

Two people. Walking away from him. Hard to see. Hard to focus. He tried to call out but his voice was as cooperative as his limbs.

He squeezed his eyes shut, opened them again, peering hard at the figures. He knew them? Knew one of them, at least… Long hair. Purple shirt. It was him. Me. Himself. No, that couldn't be right.

He was himself. Wasn't he? But he was *sure* that was him over there along the beach. So who was *he*?

Nobody important, obviously. Easiest to just lie there at the edge of the infinite ocean, and wait for the tide to come in. Let the tide wash away whatever… whatever was left. Whatever it was. He closed his eyes.

He felt the water slowly rise around him. Yes, this was easy.

Noise. Funny noise. Like a – buzzing? No, purring. Purring noise in his left ear.

He opened his eyes. Big white thing. Eyes. There were eyes – great black holes inside golden circles, in the middle of the big white thing. What did it want? Didn't matter. Easier to sleep…

Purring noise not going away. Now something was batting at his face. Paw. Cat's paw.

Cat? Kat!

Stewart's eyes snapped open. "Kat? What are you doing here?"

He shook his head, or tried to. It was like juggling a bowling ball. Kat wedged his head under the wizard's face and lifted. Interspersed with the purr was an insistent *mmrreow!*

With a considerable effort John B. raised himself up onto an elbow. The two figures that had almost disappeared into the distance suddenly seemed a bit closer. He realised that the water had ebbed. The big Persian contin-ued to headbutt him, gently but stubbornly.

His breathing labored, Stewart hauled himself to his feet. The two fig ures seemed much nearer – not like they were walking backwards but as though the ground under them had somehow slid closer. The figure in the purple shirt – it *was* him, no doubt about it.

Head spinning, John B. fell back down to his knees. Before he collapsed completely, though, he realized that Kat was staring fixedly at him.

As their gazes locked he heard the cat say very distinctly, "Don't you dare give up on me, John B. Stewart!"

It was the Persian's mouth that moved, but the voice belonged to Elizabeth Dance.

The wizard stared. Kat blinked but his gaze never wavered.

"Right then," said John B. With a surge of energy he stood up. After wavering unsteadily for a moment he gathered what was left of his wits and started to run along the sand.

He heard a much more typically feline *mrreow* behind him, and kept running towards the two figures.

One was hazy. Male but indistinct, like he was in soft focus or somehow not fully formed. The other though was now quite recognizable. It was quite definitely himself.

Uncomprehending but determined Stewart reached out and grasped his 'other' self's shoulder.

The world, or whatever it was, went white.

*

Like a slideshow controlled by a madman, images tumbled fast across the whiteness that seemed to fill Stewart's head. It was as though he was hovering, ghost-like, just above the events that spun past. Not just seeing them, but feeling them, too.

There was Dashkov's childhood in 1860's aristocratic tsarist Russia, with education in the sciences, not the more traditional arts.

He saw the Count's funeral, and the storm at the Exhibition.

There were fleeting images of the renamed Tretyakov using an experimental treatment to provide a cure for cholera – a disease that he then visited upon his oldest brother.

He was aware of Rastorguyev's fiscal struggles, and the early hope of glory that involvement in the Russo-Japanese war represented. He knew that war provided the opportunity for Tretyakov to get his brother to the front, fatally.

There - Rastorguyev observing Tretyakov's vigour as his own faded, the dying merchant convinced to name as heir in return for treatment, which was of course sabotaged.

He witnessed the selling of the inherited assets, another name switch, this time to Solovyov and the opening of French and later Swiss accounts.

Uncomfortable impressions scored across his mind of the early work with the *Cheka* in all its forms; meeting with Stalin; and the Cold War research ostensibly for the KGB. Things were done there that would shred the conscience of a good man.

Images of the puzzling new policy of *glasnost* crowded alongside those of the journey to Australia. He saw the clandestine acquisition of Mundara and remembered building the laboratory in the basement.

There were no thoughts of family. In his various guises Konstantin had been focused on extending his own existence, not living on through his progeny. He was the last of his line.

All of these and many more visions – memories – invading and filling Stewart's head, buzzing like a huge swarm of bees, finding their way into every corner.

The buzzing rose in pitch and intensity, until his head echoed with a scream. It might have been his own, or someone else's, or both.

A crackling corona of coruscating colours enveloped John B. Stewart's body. Solo may or may not have registered the extraordinary sight before the energy flew along the wires, lit up his mesh skull cup like an exploding rainbow, then raced on to the control desk.

John B.'s eyes snapped open. There was a brief loud crackle and several sharp pops. With an effort, he raised his head from the table and looked around.

In his comfortable chair, Solo looked like he was asleep, except that there was no rise and fall of his chest. Realising that he was still strapped down and so would be unable to get up from the table, John B. could do nothing to check on the scientist. Still, the wizard knew he was dead. As a massive surge of bioelectricity had ripped through him every synapse in Kon stantin Solovyov's brain had been fried, including the ones that controlled

breathing and the beating of the hundred-plus-year-old heart.

If he waited and watched long enough the wizard would see the colour

and elasticity disappear from the Russian's face, leaving his features sunk-

en, sagging and grey. There would be a striking physical resemblance to

Vladimir Dashkov – in his final hours, at least.

Stewart tried to twist his neck to see what had happened to Yusupova.

The glimpse he could catch wasn't pretty. The bioelectricity that had

coursed fatally through Dr. Solo – the amplified combination of Stewart's

and the scientist's own, had been converted to a massive discharge of con-

ventional electrical energy by the mad machines that she was operating.

She at least would be spared any aging effects on her face and figure.

Agony Aleksa, who had worked so hard to preserve the looks she had been

so proud of, was a very unattractive charred corpse.

John B. exhaled through taut lips. "I wish I could get out of this foul

room," he muttered.

The incinerated figure of Aleksandra Glafira Olga Nataliya Yusupova

toppled forward onto the control panel. Wisps of smoke from both curled

up to the laboratory ceiling, and rolled across above Stewart's head.

Fearing his own fiery demise the wizard instinctively pulled against his

restraining straps. He was surprised and delighted to find that the bioelec-

tric charge had turned the leather brittle and they snapped readily.

He rolled off the table and tried to run to the door. His legs failed him and he collapsed to the floor. The acrid smell of charred flesh was strong in his nostrils. Cursing, Stewart slapped at his legs to restore some circulation.

With an effort, he lurched to his feet and staggered to the door. It slid open onto a small vestibule fronting a steep flight of stairs. For the first time John B. realised that the laboratory had been located in a cellar.

He stumbled again and sat on a stair. He was trying to catch his breath, and try to make some sense of the images that were still tumbling through his brain.

There was a *whoosh* from the lab that he felt as much as heard, and realised that some sparks or embers from the control desk – or Aleksa's body – had ignited something.

"I'm not going back in there to fight it!" he muttered. He slid the door shut and clambered up the stairs.

He cursed again as he fumbled with the catch of the trapdoor and slid it aside.

That provoked a burst of swearing from a familiar Tasmanian voice. "What's with this house?!? Now the bloody floor moves!"

John B. couldn't help himself. He laughed. At Wilko's incongruous indignation, with relief at finding the Tasmanian still alive, as a release from escaping his own nightmare – he laughed helplessly, until tears formed in the corners of his eyes.

The wizard threw an arm around the shoulders of his old friend and, fighting to catch his breath, said, "I have *never* been so glad to see you, little buddy!"

Wilko's response to the stress of the situation wasn't laughter but irritation. He squirmed a little uncomfortably and put an awkward hand on Stewart's arm.

"Good to see you too," he said, "but my name's not Gilligan."

"Sorry mate, no offence intended." John B. had momentarily forgotten his friend's dislike of the adjective 'little' in any connection with himself.

The Tasmanian grunted acceptance of the apology, slightly mollified. He glowered at Stewart, whose laughter was being replaced by a look of agitation.

"Weird stuff happens around you, man! Weird *bad* stuff!" scolded Wilko.

John B. broke off his convivial embrace and said urgently, "You think I haven't noticed that myself? Let's get out of here – there's a fire happening in the cellar. Where's Q?"

"Cellar? There's a cellar? Who's Q?"

Elizabeth ran into the room and without a second thought threw her arms around the wizard. "John! I thought I heard your voice! You're alive!"

"Yeah, and keen to stay that way. Let's get out of here before the place burns down around us!"

"Burns…?" Now both Elizabeth and Wilko could smell the smoke starting to rise from underfoot.

As they all ran for the door John B. stopped and said, "Where's the ugly bugger?   He might deserve it but I can't let him cook…"

Elizabeth turned and met Stewart's eyes.

"He's past your saving," she said.

The wizard nodded in understanding.

"He had an unlucky accident," she continued.

Wilko, now at the front doorway, looked back and called, "The bastard was working on kicking the life out of Elizabeth."

John B. nodded again and said evenly, "So he got what he deserved, then."

Indicating the smoke rolling from the lounge room doorway as flames started up from the floor above the cellar Q grabbed his hand and said, "I think they all did, eh? Come on!"

"Right!"

The only momentary pause in their flight was for Elizabeth to pick up her bag.

"Never leave home without it," she said, quickly checking the contents.

*

They'd stood at the edge of the forest for a while, watching the house burn.

John B. had gone very quiet after puzzling Wilko by asking for a pen and any scrap of paper in his pocket. The other two had slipped cautiously a little away to give him the space he clearly wanted.

Under a sheltering tree Q watched as Stewart wrote. The lush rain-swollen foliage was in no danger of igniting so that at least was no concern. Lines of concentration on his face were thrown into stark relief by the light of the fire consuming the old Ranger's accommodation. The fire was intense. The trappings and relics of Russia's aristocratic past were incinerated alongside the mad machines that had been, in so many ways, Doctor Solo's life.

After a couple of the storms that regularly swept the island, there would be little to be found of what had been Mundara's only building, and nothing at all of its former residents.

Even after the agitation and relief of escape and being reunited with his friends, John B.'s mind was still awash with fragments of memories of the man who'd been Konstantin Dashkov, then Konstantin Tretyakov, then Konstantin Solovyov. But the fragments were disintegrating.

Among the last remaining fragments were the details of how to access the dead doctor's Swiss banked fortune.

"Okay – what do I do with this?" he mused, looking at the piece of paper on which he'd scribbled the account information before it faded, as he already felt it doing. "It's certainly not something I *wished* for."

Oddly enough, that was particularly important. It was an element of some primal ethical code that he recognised by instinct deeper than intellect.

He wrote down another number that was floating across his mindscape. It was, he realised, the current value of Solovyov's account.

"He's been drawing on it," Stewart noted. "I suppose this whole set-up can't have been cheap. Nor would keeping it quiet. Right. Well. Not *Fortune 500* stuff, but good enough. I might not have Wilko's accountancy skills but I should be able to survive on it for a while. Maybe it's time I moved on from the Public Service – I think there's something bigger out there I have to do service to. Not sure what yet, but it'll come to me. Good things come to those who wait."

Q walked over to him and asked cautiously, "Hey - how're you doing?"

John B. smiled. "It'll be alright. *I'll* be alright. Thanks."

She returned the smile. "Good. Come on, Wilko should be at the boat."

"Great. Blow in my ear and I'll follow you anywhere."

With a playful smile Q promptly blew in his ear.

.o0o.

31 ENDINGS, AND MORE

The *Helen Back* was returned to Wal without incident. The return voyage was considerably calmer than their first effort. John B. was a willing deckhand but contentedly left the 'real sailing' to Wilko and Q.

The Tasmanian, rather happier with the world as Mundara disappeared over the horizon behind them, had carefully removed any traces of Gleb's blood from the EPIRB. He didn't want to have to explain any more details than necessary to the boat's owner, not least because he really wasn't altogether sure of them himself.

As it turned out, Wal wasn't the sort of man to ask awkward questions. He was simply pleased to have *Helen* returned in good condition. Catching up with his old workmate John B. Stewart was an added bonus, although he was glad to see his clients' obvious relief at his return.

The boat owner's only question about what might have happened on Mundara was, "Is everyone okay?"

"We're all fine, thanks mate," was John B.'s reply.

There was no need to mention the three Russians who were very much not okay.

A while later, the three Canberran companions were together in the foyer of the up-market Regal Hotel. They'd agreed that the bar there was a more inviting prospect than the slightly grotty and certainly smaller one at the place Wilko and Q were staying in.

In the cab on their way there they had very quietly discussed what they should do about the island and its former inhabitants. Their driver seemed to speak little or no English but they weren't taking chances.

"It's simple," said Elizabeth. "We'll lodge a report with the police explaining that we'd been out sailing, and saw smoke coming up from the island. We landed, found the house in flames – it was too far gone for us to fight it, or even try to see if anyone was inside."

Wilko shrugged. "I don't like it, but I've got nothing better."

"We should report it to that nice Constable Iglesias," Elizabeth continued. "He's just the man to drop a mess on."

"I don't want us caught up in a bureaucratic mess," protested Wilko. "Three people died out there and I don't want that tied to us in any way!"

The wizard had maintained a contemplative silence throughout the journey.

As they'd entered the foyer he had sat down in a quiet corner and beckoned the other two close.

John B. looked thoughtful as he replied, "I don't think that you've got anything to worry about, mate," he told Wilko. "I think this will hit a desk in Canberra and very quietly disappear. No 'international incident', no investigation, no nothing. To all intents and purposes Solo and his comrades will have never been there, and neither, my friends, will we. Even if someone discovers or admits that the doctor was there, he left no heirs anyway. Whatever department Darren found that the island formerly belonged to will quietly reclaim it, with nobody to contest it."

"You're sure of that?" asked the Tasmanian.

"Yeah. Yeah, I am. Only one person alive knows much of anything about Konstantin Solovyev, and anything I didn't write down is fading fast."

"One person? Oh – you. Right. How *is* your head now?" asked Q, concerned.

"Still throbbing a bit. It felt like it was turned inside out and shaken, and I'm still putting the pieces back."

He didn't mention the strange distant buzzing that had been at the very back of his mind since the incident that had triggered his magical power. The sensation was still in place. That was vaguely comforting, he realised.

"Speaking of Darren, I must ring him! Let him know I'm okay," Stewart exclaimed.

"Good idea," agreed Elizabeth. "Here, use my phone. I'll go and talk to Mr. Cappello about a room for you – I think he owes you some consideration. Then I'll arrange our flights back to Canberra. Wilko, would you go and see if you can pull up the airline web page on that 'complimentary business terminal' over there?"

Wilko fought down the urge to salute. He knew that Elizabeth's organizational skills had really run their office for some time, even if Kaiser Ron never quite seemed to acknowledge it.

While his two friends went about their administrative tasks, Stewart rang Darren's new mobile number, hoping the young man wasn't too busy at work to answer.

He was pleased when the call was answered almost immediately.

"Hello?" came Darren's voice.

"G'day old mate! It's John B. Just landed back on the mainland and wanted to let you know I'm alive. Thanks in no small part to you, I gather…"

"Oh, mate! Mate, that's wonderful. I'm so glad!" Darren said, then paused.

The wizard could hear his housemate breathing deeply down the line. There was a definite sense, beyond the obvious relief, that something was wrong.

"What's happened? I can hear it in your voice."

Darren's reply was almost an uncomfortable stammer.

"John – oh John, I'm so sorry mate… I couldn't get in touch with you. I tried calling Wilko but his phone wasn't answering either. I…"

Stewart kept his voice steady as he said, "Slow down mate – what's wrong?"

"I'm sorry. It's Kat."

There was a long pause before the wizard broke the strained silence.

"Was it… peaceful?" he asked.

After a deep breath Darren replied, "I guess so. I saw him curled up on some open books on the floor – on the atlas, actually, before I went out shopping. I figured he was asleep."

John B. nodded, picturing the scene. "He was still there when you got home?"

"Um, yeah," said his housemate. "I didn't realise at first. When I went into the kitchen and realised his food hadn't been touched..."

The wizard sighed. "Yeah. That would be a big clue that something was wrong."

There was another long silence.

Darren said haltingly, "I... buried him under the apple blossom. He – seemed to like it there. Was that...?"

"You did good, old friend," John B. reassured him. "When did... no, wait. This would have been only this afternoon. Around lunchtime you went out, wasn't it?"

"How did you know?" was the puzzled question.

An image was in Stewart's head. A vague, dimly remembered image of a strange beach.

"I wonder if cats dream?" John B. mused softly.

"Sorry? I didn't catch that."

"Something... kind of a memory. I think he - visited me."

"Saying goodbye?" suggested the young man.

"Maybe. It's not clear. I think he was helping me? Listen, Darren – thank you. For everything you've done."

Darren tried to regain his equilibrium and sound modest as he said, "Yeah, well. I wanted to do something. It was pretty cool, actually, that research stuff. I'm thinking maybe I should have a go at studying. Computers maybe."

John B. smiled gently down the phone. "You know that whatever you want to do, I'll back you. Thanks again for... looking after Kat. I'll be home soon. Elizabeth's organising things."

"She seems very good at that," Darren replied.

"That's putting it mildly." Distressed as he was about his beloved cat, the image of Q 'taking charge' still brought a grin to Stewart's face. "See you soon, then."

"Sure thing," said his young friend. "Thanks John."

John B. pressed the 'Call End' button on the phone.

He drew a deep breath and waited for the other two to rejoin him. When they did, he quietly related the gist of his conversation with Darren. He wasn't quite successful at concealing the distress in his voice.

Wilko bit his lower lip, reached over and squeezed Stewart's shoulder. "I'm sorry mate," he said. "He was a great cat. Look, I'll go get us a round of drinks and we can raise a glass to him, eh?"

"Sounds good. Thanks," John B. said with a small smile as the Tasmanian walked away.

Elizabeth quietly took the wizard's hand.

He turned to her. "That last dream, or whatever it was. Before I came to in the lab. I don't remember much, but I know Kat was there to help me."

"That's kind of nice." She smiled. "You hear about things like that.
Bonds between people who are very close. Why not animals?"

John B. looked down at their clasped hands, then back up into Elizabeth's
eyes. Quietly he said, "You were there too."

"Was I?"

He nodded and said, "Thank you."

"I'm still here. Come on, let's save Wilko a walk with those drinks, hey?"

Exchanging smiles they walked into the bar to share a toast to old friends
and the future.

-FIN-

конец

Next: A golfing holiday in Hawaii for John B. and Wilko. What could

go wrong? Plenty, when a mysterious killer stalks the Big Island, and a

human sacrifice may have earth-shaking consequences – literally!

THE WARRIORS OF WIWO'OLE

The Fourth Book of Dubious Magic